PUFFIN BOOKS

AN ENEMY AT GREEN KNOWE

Tolly and Ping, who had had so many adventures separately at Green Knowe, are at last spending a holiday together in that beautiful and incredibly ancient house, where strange things are always happening. 'I wonder what it will be this time,' says Tolly.

They don't have to wait long to find out. On their first night Mrs Oldknow tells them the story of Dr Vogel, an alchemist who stayed at Green Knowe in the seventeenth century and got himself much too deeply involved in black magic. Next morning a letter arrives from 'Dr Melanie D. Powers', who is extremely interested in tracking down Dr Vogel's book, and soon Dr Powers herself is walking down the garden path. She seems ordinary enough – but why does she walk in that peculiar way, as though she were afraid of treading on something, and why does she avoid passing mirrors? The two boys quickly realize that they, Mrs Oldknow and the house itself are in terrible danger.

You'll need strong nerves to read this, the fifth of Lucy Boston's 'Green Knowe' tales, for the atmosphere of quiet, deadly menace which Dr Powers brings into the book is intense. But the presence of Green Knowe – welcoming and comfortable and rejoicing and gay, and full of *good* mysteries – is always felt and always re-assuring.

Lucy Boston was born in 1892 at Southport, Lancs., into a very religious family. She was one of six children and was sent to a Quaker school. She married in 1917. Interested in painting and music, she bought a delightful house in Cambridge in 1939 and ran a music club there for the R.A.F. She started writing at the age of sixty, and won the Carnegie Medal for *A Stranger at Green Knowe*. Lucy Boston died in 1990.

Other books by Lucy M. Boston

The Castle of Yew   The Children of Green Knowe
The Chimneys of Green Knowe   The River at Green Knowe
The Sea Egg   The Stones of Green Knowe
A Stranger at Green Knowe

LUCY M. BOSTON

AN ENEMY
AT GREEN KNOWE

Illustrated by Peter Boston

PUFFIN BOOKS

in association with Faber and Faber Ltd

PUFFIN BOOKS

Published by the Penguin Group
Penguin Books Ltd, 27 Wrights Lane, London W8 5TZ, England
Penguin Books USA Inc., 375 Hudson Street, New York, New York 10014, USA
Penguin Books Australia Ltd, Ringwood, Victoria, Australia
Penguin Books Canada Ltd, 10 Alcorn Avenue, Toronto, Ontario, Canada M4V 3B2
Penguin Books (NZ) Ltd, 182–190 Wairau Road, Auckland 10, New Zealand

Penguin Books Ltd, Registered Offices: Harmondsworth, Middlesex, England

First published by Faber & Faber Ltd 1964
Published in Puffin Books 1977
7 9 10 8

Copyright © Lucy Maria Boston, 1964
All rights reserved

Printed in England by Clays Ltd, St Ives plc
Set in Linotype Baskerville

To
GILES VELLACOTT
who took me to Fydlyn and
CLAIRE RYLE
who asked me for a tale about the
Persian looking-glass

NOTE

'Crossing the River' is the real name of one of several traditional languages used by witches. I have seen the alphabet, but do not know what letters the signs represent. I have used it as it suited me for the purposes of this book and offer my apologies to any person reading it who is familiar with the language and knows the correct usage.

Tolly and Ping, his Chinese friend, just back from a camping holiday, were emptying out of their haversacks the pebbles that they could not bear to leave behind. Their camp had been close to the sea, and they had collected palm-fitting stones as they walked on the tide-washed beaches, every day discarding some and adding others. Now the stones lay in a heap on the lawn at Green Knowe while Tolly poured water over them to bring out the colour and sparkle. The brightest were of green or blood-red marble, and for contrast black basalt figured with white, or semi-transparent eggs of amber or moonstone which felt to the fingers like velvet stroked along the pile.

Ping turned the pebbles over lovingly and handed his favourites to Mrs Oldknow. 'Stones ought to be magic,' he said, 'they fit your hand *too* well. It feels as though they meant something important.'

'They are the natural weapons,' the old lady answered, teasing. 'Wild man would be very good at throwing them at things. Natural tools, too – the first nutcrackers and all that. Perhaps it's just your primitive instincts coming out.'

'It doesn't make me feel at all like Wild Man. It makes me feel wise, as if I knew things. Only I don't know what it is I know.'

'They were used in Magic, too,' she said, relenting.

'If we had to choose one stone for doing magic with, which would we choose?' asked Tolly. He picked out a pale green oval for all the world like a snatch of surf turned into stone, foam flecks and all. 'How would this be for walking on water?'

Ping was engrossed with a flat oval of slate subtly ringed with white veins, which he was following with his finger. The surface had a rough drag like a kitten's tongue. The rings went round and round the stone, pivoted at a slight angle, growing smaller and smaller till they ended in nothing. 'This would be for disappearing. You get smaller and smaller till pff! you are gone. It would be more useful than walking on the water. At least it would be useful oftener. And look, Grand Mother, I brought this back specially for you, because it was a pity you weren't there. It has a hole in it. You could wear it round your neck.'

This one was a polished flat pear shape in the blackest possible black. The hole was near the top, smooth and big enough for Ping's little finger. The lower part was figured with a white star and some intricate mathematical-looking curves, made of course not by man, but by the sky and the sea and the earth all working together.

'What a wonderful thing! Where did you find it, Ping?'

'In Fydlyn Bay. During the storm, when the tide was up, the waves were boiling with stones and throwing them about like spray, and afterwards the shore was quite a different shape. Instead of being all even, it was a great bank of rocks and stones at one side and a great hollow at the other.'

'Fydlyn! I know it well. That is where the last of the Druids were driven into the sea by the Romans. The Chief Druid used to wear a Stone of Power round his neck. I can imagine the storm churning up the bottom

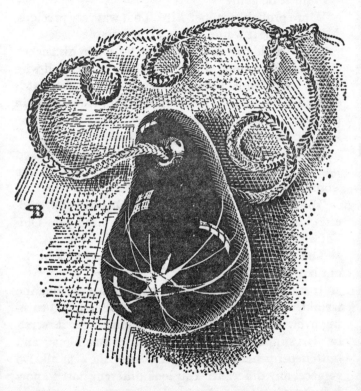

of the bay, rolling great rocks up and down deep under the water, shifting the base of cliffs, splitting open cracks and throwing up far on the shore things that had lain hidden for two thousand years. This *could* be the Druid's stone. I wonder who would know. I wonder if one of them has ever been found. I imagine there would only be one. It would not be buried with him, it would be handed on to his successor.'

'What would it be threaded on?' asked Tolly, standing with his arm round his great-grandmother's neck. 'Would it be gold?'

'More probably copper wire. That was very precious. I don't think it would be very comfortable.'

'How would this do?' said Ping, fishing in his pocket. 'I found a lot of long silvery horsehair in a barbed-wire fence. Its tail must have been terribly knotted to catch so badly. We used to learn straw and grass weaving in the hostel, so I amused myself by weaving a bit of horsehair ribbon. It's very strong.'

It was about a quarter of an inch wide and looked like coarse silver thread. Ping passed it through the stone.

'We hereby make you head of all Druids and Druidesses,' he said, putting the two ends round Mrs Oldknow's neck. 'Tie it, Tolly.'

The two boys sat back on their heels to look at the old lady.

'It suits you,' said Tolly. 'Your wrinkles are like the wrinkles on sand, when the waves have laughed turning over. They do sometimes. You must wear it secretly.' He slipped it inside the collar of her blouse and buttoned up her cardigan. 'It doesn't show at all. Do you feel any different? You look different now I know it is there.'

'You two!' she said lovingly. 'As soon as either of you comes I know I am in for something. Come in now, you've had a long journey.'

Ping and Tolly raced into the house, glad to be there again. It was Tolly's own, in that it was his great-

grandmother's, while it was Ping's only by adoption, but they loved it equally and Mrs Oldknow made no difference between them. Perhaps she allowed herself to be more demonstrative to Tolly because he was her own, and because Ping was Chinese and reserved; but Ping understood that perfectly. He never could quite bring himself to the familiarity of Granny, but called her Grand Mother in two words. When Tolly spoke of her to Ping he called her Grand.

'I'm glad this house is stone,' said Tolly. 'It smells of stone. When you come back to any house that you know, it has such a special smell. Do you think when they built this they put in some magic somewhere to make it last? Because it has lasted so much longer than houses do.'

'I am sure they did – or something magic. It was a custom going right back to the first houses ever made. Generally it was something under the threshold, or on the roof, or perhaps under the hearth – the three most important places.'

'Have you looked?' Tolly was patting and stroking the walls as if they were alive.

'No,' the old lady said. 'I haven't disturbed anything. Whatever is there is working very well.'

Ping smiled and said nothing.

'You are sleeping together in the attic,' she went on, 'but we'll have supper before you go up.'

'I must go and look at it again,' said Tolly. 'It is too long since I saw it. Come on, Ping.'

They went larking off up the steep wooden stairs, across the Music Room or Knights' Hall as Tolly called it, and up the still steeper and narrower stairs to their attic. They hung out of the windows to see the garden, the river, the islands, the birds. They bounced on the beds, listened to the old clock, rattled the familiar drawer handles, and Ping picked up meditatively a large green flagon that his friend Oscar had once found in the river.

In the camp he and Tolly had shared a tent, and alone in it at night, with the stars showing through the opening, they had told each other the almost un-believable things that had happened to them separately at Green Knowe. At last they were there together. To both of them it was now home, and also the most won-derful place on earth. It was like nowhere else, because while most houses are built to shut out everything but the inmates, to close doors and draw curtains equally against the cold winds from the edge of space and the

14

curiosity of the neighbours, to make a cosy den where everything is yours and under your control, Green Knowe was full of mysteries. Certainly it was welcoming and comfortable and rejoicing and gay, but one had the feeling that behind the exciting colours and shapes of its ancient self there might be surprises from the unknown universe; that the house was on good terms with that too, and had no intention of shutting out the un-understandable. Of course, it was largely Time. Surely Now and Not-now is the most teasing of all mysteries, and if you let in a nine-hundred-year dose of time, you let in almost everything.

Tolly looked at Ping, whose adventures here had been so different from his own.

'I wonder what it will be this time,' he said. 'Come on, let's go down and start.'

After supper, in spite of their long journey, the boys were still unwilling to go to bed. They had only just arrived and had hardly had time to realize they were there.

'Let's just go and look at the river,' said Tolly.

It was a soft warm night with a Hunter's Moon just rising. It was Ping who had had so many adventures on the river, and as he looked now at the golden ribbon of water with the dark trees reflected upside down in it, his thoughts were far away. Then he heard Tolly saying to Mrs Oldknow, 'If we went to bed now, we should only stay awake looking out of the window. Anyone would. Let's sit in the garden and you tell us a story, just to start the holiday off. And we can watch the moon go up. Besides, it smells so wonderful.'

'I'm glad you're not too old for stories,' the old lady

said, as they set their deck-chairs opposite the moon-rise and let themselves become part of the quiet dusk. 'I like talking about the house and the people who lived here. I have spent my life collecting odd bits of gossip and local legend.'

'The queer thing about Granny's stories,' Tolly explained to Ping, 'is that bits of them keep coming true *now*, although they are all so old.'

Ping came out of his reverie.

'Do you know anything about someone called Piers Madeley?' he asked. 'When Oscar and I were staying here that summer when you were away, we found a big green bottle in the rushes with a long confession in it, written by him. Only we couldn't read it.'

'How odd that you should ask about Piers Madeley! I was thinking about him only today. I was in that room by the front door, you know, the room we don't use much, dusting the big witchball, when its string broke. If I hadn't been holding it it would have been looking-glass-powder by now. Well, never mind about the witchball. I'll show it you later.'

THE STORY OF DR VOGEL

In 1630, the lord of the Manor of Green Knowe, Squire Oldknow, had a son, Roger, about nine years old, who was a clever boy but consumptive, so that he could not be sent away to school. This was a great disappointment to his parents, who wished him to go to the University. Piers Madeley, the Vicar, had taught him from the time when he was old enough to learn, and now had come to the end of what little Latin and Greek he knew himself. Piers was a good soul, well liked and faithful, but no scholar, as he himself confessed.

One day Squire Oldknow came back from Greatchurch and announced that he had found an excellent tutor for Roger – a famous scholar and Alchemist called Dr Vogel. This eminent person would teach Roger Latin and Greek and Mathematics in return for his board and lodging and the use of sundry outhouses and rooms where he could carry out his many studies and experiments. He could have the vaults under the ruined Chapel for his furnaces and a room in the house for his study. Mistress Oldknow must see that the servants treated him with the respect due to a great man, not a mere tutor like good Piers.

There was great excitement in the house, of course, at the idea of having such a person to live with the family. Roger, who was the one most affected, asked repeatedly, 'What is he like?' But Squire Oldknow had not even seen him. He had accepted the recommendation of a friend.

'I am told he is a very fine man,' he assured his wife, 'handsome in his dress and manner, which is unusual in one so devoted to learning. Look at the letter he wrote to me. It has a magnificent style.'

The letter led off with the words:

Most honoured Sir

inscribed with an exuberance of squirls, loops and whiplashes from which the words themselves could only be disentangled by guesswork. The body of the letter was in a more moderate style and could be read with determination, but from time to time the letters were seized with a burst of energy and spurted up with interlacing spirals like flames from a smouldering fire. As for the signature, it was, to Roger's eyes, monstrous. It was written with a special quill, to make the wrestling match between loops and downstrokes, enrichments, returns and underlinings, as strong and black as ink could make it. His first name of Wolfgang gave him special opportunities, as you will see if you try.

'Would you not wonder,' said Squire Oldknow to his son, 'that a man could write so fine a hand?'

Roger looked at it with apprehension but thought it might be fun to try what one could do oneself in that line.

'I would rather have our vicar's simple lettering,' said Mistress Oldknow, 'even if his spelling is as homely as himself. This other man will be too grand for the house.'

'Ah no, my dear. He will teach our son manners as well as the classics.'

'I hope he will not teach him to write so that I cannot read his letters.'

The squire was still looking at the paper with astonished delight.

'These scholars are remarkable men for writing. And they can read each other's letters too.'

The day came when Roger was presented to his future master. He saw a tall deep-chested man with long unruly black hair, tufted eyebrows and a great deal of black beard. Within the curls of his beard could be seen a very small, very red mouth. His nose was prominent and pointed. It pointed almost as much as his long first finger, which – in spite of the courtly play of his hands unruffling his lace cuffs, touching his heart, trifling with his cravat, gesturing like a Frenchman – seemed constantly to be pointing at something admired, despised, coveted or commanded. It was all the more fascinating to watch the movements of that accusing and acquisitive finger, because his eyes were elsewhere. They had a slight outward cast and when they wandered it was not in the same direction as his finger.

The mixed feelings of shyness and excitement with which Roger had looked forward to this moment were suddenly simplified into dislike.

Dr Vogel's arrival was followed by a wagon containing all the apparatus of his profession – the globes, astrolabe, maps, telescope, crucibles, vats, cauldrons, metal ores and herbs. Some of the books were so big they had to be carried in one at a time. And there was a box of snakes. Mrs Oldknow would not allow that into the house. It was put in the chapel vault in a corner near the new furnace.

This was a time when people were terrified of witchcraft and everybody believed in it. Yet to be an Alchemist, to try to brew the elixir of life or turn lead into gold, or call up spirits and Powers, even the dead, to question them, was not considered wrong. It was much as it is today, when it is a highly respectable occupation to study nuclear fission or experiment on animals, but an envious woman in a village who should put a pinch of weedkiller in her neighbour's asters would rouse ruthless passions. Many magical formulae had been handed down from King Solomon, and even Popes and bishops studied them. The incantations read like unfamiliar parts of the Prayer Book, using all the most ancient names of God.

However, nobody was ever more popular for being thought to have a spirit in attendance. Dr Vogel cut a splendid figure in his rich clothes and doctor's gown, surrounded by learned company, and warmed with wine and feasting, for he was an imposing personality and a clever talker. Anyone who ventured to argue with him was sure to be made to look foolish. Many learned men from Greatchurch came to talk with him—so that Squire Oldknow was proud to have such a celebrated man in his house, though it cost him a lot in entertainment. His wife was increasingly displeased. She said he caused endless work and never gave a word of thanks. And good Piers Madeley, vicar of Penny Sokey, left the house after an hour spent with Dr Vogel shaking his head and saying, 'Blessed are the poor in spirit.'

The servants who saw the visitor so honoured in the Hall, saw him also at work in his vault, wearing only vest and long hose while he stirred his mixtures, dissected dead dogs or fed live frogs and mice to his snakes. They feared his fierce black eyes with their outward cast. Whichever eye you met was brilliant, but you weren't sure if that was the one he was looking at you with. Then suddenly the two would be swivelled into focus and the effect was of being held like a specimen between tweezers. His language when interrupted was hair-raising. There was a great deal of whispering among the servants.

Roger, too, was disconcerted by those independently moving eyes. But the lessons were much less stern than they might have been. In those days schoolboys were harshly treated. No allowance at all was made for youth. The more discipline the better. Dr Vogel was on the whole a negligent teacher. He was busy with his own reading or writing or charts of stars, wearing glasses that magnified his roving eyes to the size of a horse's. His quill as he wrote gave loud squawks. He gave Roger a Greek or Latin book to read and left him to it. Roger had no companion to play with or to idle with. To sit doing nothing was more tedious than to work. He knew enough of the languages to be able to read with some guesswork. Even when he was made to read aloud or construe, Dr Vogel only gave him the occasional attention of one eye; or when he made a mistake the long first finger would be lifted from its following of the print in a huge tome to be pointed momentarily at him. The finger in fact was often used when the eyes had given no sign.

The so-called lessons were no hardship. It was only when he looked up from his work to find both Dr Vogel's eyes fixing him that he felt a kind of cold pang. As time went on the Doctor's mannerisms occupied more and more of his attention. He did such odd things that Roger felt he had to watch, to see how often they happened. When he came into the room, for instance, and Roger stood up to greet him, the Doctor held the door open and looked down before he closed it, as if a little person or an animal were following him in. And sometimes when he was deep in one of his books of diagrams and breathing heavily as if in excitement, he would twitch one shoulder and say, 'Leave me alone.' And sometimes that finger would point not at Roger, but at empty space, and be meaningfully wagged.

*

Mrs Oldknow paused and for a moment they all sat silent. They watched the flight of the bats zigzagging, reversing and zooming, seen only as rapid blurs in the new night, but etched sharply, black and detailed, when they passed in front of the moon. On a branch of the acacia tree two young owls were sitting side by side. Now and again one would turn and give its fierce baby cry. The moon had just cleared the distant trees. It looked too heavy to rise any farther and was the colour of a tangerine. The garden seemed to be waiting.

After a while (Mrs Oldknow continued) things began to go wrong, things that no one could explain. Dogs howled in the yards and were found dead in the morning. Cottages that used at night to show a friendly lighted room to the village street were now shuttered close after dark. The men went to the taverns more than usual, but waited for company on the way home. On such a night as tonight, Dr Vogel had been seen gathering herbs, or moths, or snakes, on the big water meadows. *He was not alone.* You couldn't rightly tell what it was. It could have been a white hare larger than life. It ran in circles. It danced upright and made sudden swoops.

Gradually the stories got worse. It was said that a man all muffled up in a hood had come to a poor woman whose baby had been still-born and had tried to buy its body for a piece of gold. Everybody knew dead bodies were needed for black magic – for the worst kind.

It was a very hot summer. Cooped indoors with his tutor, Roger's illness became noticeably worse. His parents thought that perhaps the discipline was too

severe, and they asked Dr Vogel to spare the boy and remember he was an invalid. This resulted in the Doctor's taking a new interest very unwelcome to Roger – an over-kindness that compressed his little red mouth into a parody of an old maid's. Sometimes he would lean in mock fatherliness on Roger's shoulder as he was bent over his writing, and then give a sharp shove as if to test how much resistance there was in the boy. This generally brought on a fit of desperate coughing.

'None too good, my poor boy. None too good,' he would say as he went back to his place, rubbing his hands nervously. 'None too good, is he?' he added, to no one who was there.

Roger was clearly getting worse every week. He was thin, with a high feverish colour, and too excitable. He implored his mother with tears to take him away from Dr Vogel. His parents thought it was hysteria due to his illness. They saw no reason for him to be frightened, but then they never saw what Dr Vogel did when they were not there, nor how his rolling eyes suddenly focused on poor Roger with impatient glee, as if to say, 'It won't be long now.' The servants said another dead body was wanted.

However, Roger's terror at last reached such a pitch that his parents took him away to stay with his grandmother in Devon, hoping the change of air would do him good. She was glad to have him and pleaded for him to be left with her. His mother and father took the long journey home without him. They had been away a month – such journeys were not lightly undertaken – and when they had set out there had been no idea of leaving Roger behind; in which case Dr Vogel would have been told his duties were over, though it might have been difficult to get rid of him.

On their return they found Green Knowe in confusion. Dr Vogel had disappeared, leaving all his possessions behind, except his books, as you shall hear.

A week after Roger had been taken away, Dr Vogel sent word to Piers Madeley to come to him urgently, and not to let anything stand in the way, for the love of God. Piers Madeley was afraid of Dr Vogel for every reason. He made him feel a nobody, ill-born, poor, stupid, provincial and unwanted. Yet Piers had a strong feeling that the scholar, though terrifying, was a hollow man. The wording of the message was such as a parish priest could not ignore, so although it was infinitely against his inclination, he went to Green Knowe.

He found Dr Vogel in a lamentable state, hardly recognizable. He had had no sleep for nights on end. He was unbrushed and his clothes were torn as if from a fight. He said he wished to make a confession, and as he stammered it out he behaved as if the room were full of threatening enemies, instead of containing just the two of them and the door locked. What the Doctor confessed to has of course never been told, but Piers afterwards told the Bishop that the sweat poured off him even as he listened. When he had heard it, he urgently besought Dr Vogel to burn his books and certain of his belongings. At first the unhappy man refused. His books were worth a fortune. They were also the foundation of his career, his future and his hopes of making gold. To burn them was like burning himself. But later, looking round him with a face of terror, he gave a great cry and said, 'Yes, and quickly.'

The books were upstairs indoors, and the furnace in the vaults, so to save time in carrying, they made a bonfire in the courtyard. They had to work like devils to collect all that was to be burnt. Dr Vogel repeatedly cried out, 'Make haste! Before the moon rises,' and he poured pitch and tallow into the fire. It went up like a beacon. The servants watched in terror, peeping through the windows and keeping well out of the way. If you have ever tried to burn a book, you will know it is difficult. The pages remain in a solid block and will not catch. Once Dr Vogel saw in the firelight a book lying open and unburnt, showing a page of intricate diagrams, and he let out a scream and pitchforked it into the heart of the flames. Finally there was nothing but a glowing mass. The Doctor sank exhausted on the threshold of the vault, his head in his hands. Piers managed to say a compassionate, 'Now peace be with you as your trust is in God,' and puffing painfully and mopping his brow he prepared to set off home.

'Alas!' groaned Dr Vogel, pointing at the smouldering books and looking not less woeful because his exhausted eyes were straying separately. 'What's thought cannot be unthought.'

The rim of the full moon was just rising above the trees when Piers left. It was a strange sultry colour seen through the earth mists, and opposite it in the heart of the night the crimson smoke of the bonfire went straight up like a signal. The shadows on the footpath felt to Piers almost solid. He zigzagged to avoid them, feeling his way through a gathering invisible crowd. He said his prayers aloud as he went.

Two hours later, chiding himself for his shaking knees and lack of faith he opened his bedroom win-

dow and looked out. The moon was high, the night soundless. He listened, turning his ear towards Green Knowe across the meadows. Then he heard a scream. He knew it was a man, but it was so high and throbbing it might have been a terrified horse.

There was a pause, while the boys fidgeted and the moon shone coldly.

'Nothing more was ever heard of Dr Vogel.'

'I'm glad he's dead,' said Tolly, rubbing his shin with the sole of the other foot. 'I hope he hasn't left anything behind.'

'I don't much like the idea "What's thought can't be unthought",' said Ping.

Mrs Oldknow looked at them and laughed at their nervousness.

'Do you two feel any readier to go to sleep now? It's time to go in.'

'Oh,' they said standing close together.

The entrance hall was delightfully enclosing and reassuring, full as always of flowers and birds' nests, the lights relayed from mirror to mirror all down its length, and all the scatter of happy living – secateurs, baskets, books, letters and anything-to-hand lying on the tables. The coloured stairs led up invitingly, but to get to the attic you had to pass through the Knights' Hall, which, if it had been alone for some hours, had a habit of slipping back to its own century. However much you loved it, Tolly thought, it always needed a little resolution to break away into its privacy at night.

'You didn't tell us anything about the witchball,' he reminded Mrs Oldknow, to postpone the moment. 'May we see it, please?'

The witchball was hanging from the middle beam of the room nearest the front door. It was made of looking-glass and had a diameter of about eighteen inches. The glass was old and the silvering was old. It did not glitter like modern glass, but reflected in an almost velvety way. Being round, what it reflected was a spherical room, something difficult to look at because impossible to imagine. There were no straight lines at all, no right angles. Floor, ceiling, doors, windows, tables and chairs all curved softly around its shape. Ping and Tolly, standing underneath looking up at it, appeared to be diving out of it face first, their bodies foreshortened and tapering, like tadpoles.

'You see,' said Mrs Oldknow, 'it reflects everything, even what is behind it, though that for some reason is upside down, which is supposed to be how our eyes really see things.'

'What is it used for, Granny?'

'Is it for seeing the future?'

'It looks as though it should be. You could easily see strange things in a spherical mirror-room where even ordinary things look so queer. Something could be there for quite a long time before you noticed it. Besides, it's always easier to see visions in a glass than in reality. But I believe it was supposed to keep away demons. I don't know why. Perhaps because if anyone had an attendant demon and came anywhere near the witchball they would risk the demon being seen. You must admit it looks magic enough for anything.'

'You would have to learn how to look into it,' said Tolly sensibly. 'It is difficult to recognize things in it, especially upside down.'

'A demon, if there was one,' said Ping, 'wouldn't

like being reflected, even if no one saw. It might steal some of his power.'

'I'm sure that's right, Ping,' said the old lady. 'Unlike ghosts who want to be seen and use looking-glasses to do it.'

'I suppose that is why you have so many glasses in the hall,' said Tolly. 'I like the house-ghosts too. But I think I would be happier tonight if the witchball was hanging in our bedroom. May we take it up? I don't want any of Dr Vogel's companions clutching at me.'

Mrs Oldknow laughed. 'Don't tell me you have sold your soul so young! I am counting on you to be one of the stalwart guardians of the place. You should be clutching demons by the tail, not they you.'

'Green Knowe doesn't need guardians,' said Tolly, showing in his face how proud he was of it. 'It *can't* have any enemies.'

'It has enemies and it needs guarding all the time,' said the old lady. 'In spite of all the Preservation Societies it wouldn't be there another five years if we stopped watching and guarding it. The very fact that it has lasted so long makes some people impatient. Time it went, they say, without further argument. The fact that it is different from anywhere else, with memories and standards of its own, makes quite a lot of people very angry indeed. Things have no right to be different. Everything should be alike. Over and above all the rest, it seems to me to have something I can't put a name to, which always has had enemies. Lift the witchball down. Tolly. We'll take it up to the attic. It is wasted in my workroom. It really is a beauty.'

They carried it carefully upstairs and hung it from

a beam. It was a great addition. It reflected both Ping and Tolly in their beds, though even when they sat up and waved their arms it was difficult to find themselves in it. One is not used to seeing one's self feet upwards.

At breakfast next morning, as they sat discussing what they should do on their first day, the post arrived with a letter for Mrs Oldknow. Tolly watched her read it, because he knew that she either smiled with all her wrinkles if it was from someone she liked, or tut-tutted like an annoyed wren if it was tiresome. This time she tutted and laughed.

'Here's someone who is going to waste her time and ours. Listen. It's from Dr Melanie D. Powers, Doctor of Philosophy of Geneva.

Dear Mrs Oldknow,

I have been commissioned to write a book about English private libraries in the seventeenth century. I am also acting on behalf of the Library of the Philosophical Society of Jerusalem, who are anxious to obtain certain very rare old manuscripts. One of them is thought to have been in the collection of Dr Wolfgang Vogel, who inhabited Green Knowe from 1630 until his death the following year. There is no record of his books after that date. It seems possible that some are still in your house. If so, and if you are willing to part with them, I am authorized by the Philosophical Society to arrange the price with you. As I am in the neighbourhood, I will call tomorrow about four o'clock and hope it will not be inconvenient to you. Perhaps you will be kind enough to let me see your very interesting house.

Yours sincerely,

MELANIE D. POWERS

If she had bothered to look it up in the Rolls,' said the old lady, 'she would have known the books were burnt. Piers Madeley's evidence was taken down before the magistrates when inquiries were being made about Dr Vogel's disappearance. Because other scholars wanted his books, and it was not known for certain that he was dead. However, we will let Miss Powers come, she can get some local colour for her account of Dr Vogel.'

'There you are, Ping!' Tolly exclaimed. 'Didn't I tell you part of Grannie's stories always comes true? She no sooner mentions Dr Wolfgang Vogel than Dr Melanie D. Powers comes asking about him. I wonder if she has a roving eye.'

'Or a horrible long first finger.'

Tolly then wanted to know whose the witchball was, and how it came to be there. If it was there when Dr Vogel was in the house it didn't seem to have done much good.

'No,' she answered, 'it came much later than that. But old stories and fears have long lives. You can imagine Dr Vogel was a bogey to frighten naughty children with for many generations. I heard a woman not long ago say to a screaming child, "The Old Fogey will get you if you don't stop." I'm sure that was an echo of Dr Vogel. And witches keep cropping up. There was old Petronella who put the spell on Green Noah, and Mme Magda who gave Maria Oldknow the spell for sewing with human hair. Looking-glass was invented in the early seventeenth century. It came from Italy. At first it was only in palaces and very big houses – small pieces of glass in very large embossed gold frames. But every woman wanted one and soon most houses had at least a small one. You remember, Tolly, that Toby and Alexander had an elder brother who was a sailor. His wife collected looking-glasses as other people collect china or firearms or pictures.'

'There aren't any in here,' said Tolly, looking round the living-room.

'Well, of course a lot were lost in the fire in 1799. They are not the sort of thing you can throw out of a window in a hurry. But the witchball survived. It was a treasured possession. It came from Holland. And there is a very old Persian looking-glass in the Knights' Hall. I always think there must be something special about it. But I've never caught it doing anything odd.'

'Come on, Ping, I know the one she means. May we take it down, Granny?'

'The usual answer. Yes, my dear, but *be careful*.'

The two boys went up to the Knights' Hall, or Music Room, whichever you chose to call it. It was a very high room. The walls were bare warm stone, broken only by deep-set arched windows. There were no pictures and only one looking-glass which was propped on a ledge against the sloping wall of the chimney stack, just above eye-level.

The glass could have been spanned by a man's hand, but it was set in a wide red lacquer frame. The frame itself was studded with small pieces of looking-glass set in it as part of the decoration, all tilted at slightly different angles. It gave the impression that all these bits were exploring the surrounding space on behalf of the main glass which was fixed. The frame was leaning back against the wall so that the glass looked upward, but by standing back a little the boys could see reflected in it the big rose-red Chinese lantern that hung in the middle of the room.

'What lovely reds,' said Tolly. 'The frame, one lantern in the room and another in the looking-glass. Why do reflected things always look more mysterious?'

'Tolly?' Ping was looking puzzled. 'Tolly, look at the lantern in the glass. You see how it is swinging, very slightly, in the draught? Now look at the real one. It is hanging quite still.'

'It often does swing,' said Tolly. 'Especially in the winter when the heaters and candles are on and the warmth is rising. I've often noticed it.'

'But it isn't swinging now.'

'No, it isn't.'

They both stood silent for a while, looking from the mirror to the lantern and back. A tortoiseshell butterfly flew round the real lantern and perched on its painted chrysanthemum. There was no butterfly in the mirror.

'All I can think,' said Ping at last, 'is that this glass reflects the right place but at another time.'

'It only reflects the ceiling half of the room where nothing goes on, so it could be ages before anyone noticed,' Tolly agreed.

'The question is, does it reflect the past or the future?'

'It will be the past, in this house.'

'Lift it down, Tolly, and let's look at it properly.'

They lifted it down and propped it on a chair seat, kneeling down to look in it. It showed their two interested faces cheek by cheek and their arms round each other's shoulders, and that filled up the whole surface.

'Well, that's now at any rate,' said Tolly.

'How do you know? It may be the next time we look in it.'

'Mirror, mirror on the wall
Who is the cleverest of us all?'

sang Tolly, teasingly pushing Ping over. Their mock fight ended with their tumbling one at each side of the mirror. From there, each boy saw in it a woman's face. It was colourless, and like a sculptured saint's head on a cathedral porch. But this face had an evil sneer, as shocking as if the expression of one of the gargoyles had strayed on to the face of the Madonna. It was there for so short a time they were left wondering if they had imagined it. Of course they looked round the room. There were two sculptured heads behind them on the Norman fireplace, but not at all like the one they had seen. These were restful and gravely smiling.

'Lordy!' said Tolly, sitting down with a bump. 'To think I said I liked ghosts!'

Ping was looking thoughtful, but his face was never without a certain impish resolution.

'I don't think that was a ghost. I had a feeling it didn't mean to be seen. Suppose the glass shows the future, just suppose. What I think is, if that person is coming here, it would be better to take the glass up to our room, where nobody ever comes. It would be better if she didn't know we knew in advance. It's always better with dangerous people.'

'But if we could see her, wouldn't she have seen us? You can't help that in mirrors.'

'But when she actually comes, the mirror won't be there, see? At least I hope that will be all right.'

They took the Persian glass up the wooden stairs

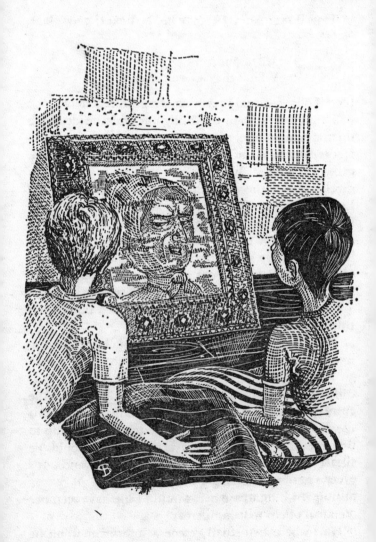

that led from the big room to their attic. They stood it on the chest of drawers behind the china dog and the ebony mouse. They looked at it a long time, but it innocently reflected the window and part of the water meadows in the distance. In the foreground instead of the Chinese lantern it now showed the witchball.

They then spent some time lovingly rearranging their treasures. Tolly had the deer's collar and a model of the frigate *Woodpecker*. Ping had Piers Madeley's green glass flagon, a map of islands and a large photo, given him by the keeper of Hanno the gorilla, whom Ping had sheltered and fed in the thickets of Green Knowe after his escape from the zoo. He also had a Burmese prayer bell that he had found in a deserted jungle temple and brought to England with him. They each had a collection of stones from Anglesey. The witchball and the Persian glass they had in common.

'What a lot of strange things we are collecting in here! I wonder what next.'

'What next' was becoming Tolly's personal motto. 'Let's go down and help Grand, and then we'll do the garden.'

'Doing the garden' meant going all round, following every path, showing each other exactly where every single thing had happened, swarming over the fallen tree that had been Hanno's bridge across the moat, climbing all the trees, looking at Green Knowe from every possible vantage-point and loving it every minute. As Ping was forest-born he was able to compete on equal terms with Tolly, who knew all the trees and holds. If Tolly swung in the top fork of the giant beech tree from which he got the best view of Green Knowe as a Norman building, singing sea shanties at the top of his voice, Ping in a tall pear tree in the orchard from which he could see the circle of the moat and the course of the river, answered with strange and distant Chinese songs. In this duet all the birds joined with enthusiasm.

They were at home.

Mrs Oldknow had the art of making every meal an informal party. Perhaps it was because she was much alone, so that having the two boys really was a party for her, of which she enjoyed every minute every time, and that was infectious. In many houses meal-times are the wrangling point, where young and old gang up against each other, boys against girls, familiars against strangers, and every grievance is aired and even exercised. In Green Knowe it was not at all like that. Tolly might have teased Ping for being Chinese, Ping might have been jealous of Tolly for being the grandson of the house, both might have disbelieved and belittled each other's adventures. The two boys might have laughed at Mrs Oldknow for her old lady's ways. She might have felt they made a lot of work and were a tiresome pair of young things. Instead, they were three quite different people who loved being together and used their imagination for laughing and devising pleasures. Each was ready to take up the others' ideas. But Mrs Oldknow always seemed to enjoy most what could be understood without actually saying it.

'Grand Mother, the Persian glass did seem rather odd, so we took it up to our attic to watch it better. Do you mind?'

'Oh no. I should like to know what its habits are, I

38

never found out. But you know I'm not really tall enough to see in it where it was, perched up there.'

The afternoon passed as pleasantly as the morning. The boys had forgotten there was to be a visitor for tea, until they saw Mrs Oldknow laying cups and plates for four.

'Who's coming, Granny?'

'Miss Powers. Had you forgotten? There, I heard the gate click.'

A person who would have passed unnoticed in any crowd anywhere was approaching along the garden path. At first sight the only individual thing about her was her way of walking. It was neither striding nor tripping nor quietly stepping, but rather as though each foot went separately without fixed rhythm. They seemed to be searching for the right place to come down, but having found it came down heavily. Children often go along the pavement like that, observing rules to tread only, or never, on cracks between the stones. But this was on plain gravel.

'What is she doing?' said Tolly. 'Is she treading on beetles?'

'Or walking to poetry?' Ping suggested. 'They call it feet, but it never goes comfortably to walking, I've often tried.'

'I think it's only a very absent-minded way of walking. Perhaps she doesn't know what to say when she meets us. Let us go and meet her.' Mrs Oldknow opened the door and waited for the visitor with a smile.

'Miss Powers? I'm Mrs Oldknow. Do come in. Did you find the house easily?'

'Oh yes, thank you. I know my way about quite well. As a matter of fact I am living in The Firs just across the next field. I have rented it for three months while I do my research on this district.'

'Oh, then we are neighbours,' Mrs Oldknow replied pleasantly, but the boys knew that this was not her most pleased voice. 'Do come in,' she repeated, standing aside to let Miss Powers pass. 'This is my great-grandson Tolly, and our friend Ping.'

The visitor began a sweet smile for the boys, but as they stood back for her, she looked down the entrance hall and saw the three backs of her hosts in the mirror that faced the door. The smile faded away, but as quickly returned.

'Why,' she said, in a laughing apologetic way, 'this is the newest part of the house. Wouldn't it be more dramatic to walk round and come in at the oldest part, for my first entry? I am very susceptible to old houses and don't want to lose a single thrill. Every old house is like a love-affair to me. And this one, I know, is going particularly to enmesh me. I shall never be the same again.'

All this time she was backing away and turning off to go round the side of the house. She had a slow, soft, very considered voice, and though what she said was too much, the confidence with which she said it was imposing, so that even Mrs Oldknow fell in with her suggestion, though surprised to find someone so ready to do the honours of the house for herself.

'Oh yes!' the visitor went on, 'here are the famous Norman windows, and the wonderful old front, with the date of the fire up there in the plaster. Boys, do you never imagine someone watching you out of these windows? A face perhaps with a roving eye?' She cascaded in soft laughter. 'No, I see I can't frighten you. You are much too sensible. Well, here it is, all just as I imagined it when I read of it. It feels like coming home.' She put her hand on the door-knob, and then withdrew it as if someone had interfered. She looked round and saw the statue of St Christopher in his shower of Traveller's Joy, which just now was a foam of tiny white flowerets.

'Oh dear!' she said with a half laugh. 'Gentlemen like that should be in churches where one expects to find them. They are surprising in gardens. Do, do please ask me to come in quickly. I can't wait to see it all.'

Mrs Oldknow opened the door silently and showed her in. Inside the door two steps led down to the level of the old living-room floor, so that anyone coming in had a particular impression of stepping right into something different. Most strangers paused here to adjust themselves to the unexpectedness of the house. Its atmosphere was as certain and permanent as the smell and sound of the sea in a shell. No one could miss it.

Miss Powers had come across the threshold with a look almost of triumph, but once there, she stood breathing quickly and seemed to have more difficulty than most people in taking the measure of it. Then she clasped her hands.

'What a *thrilling* room! And what a fireplace! Yes, you can really see out of the top of the chimney. And here's the cauldron hook! Would this be where Dr Vogel had his furnace? If he failed to make the elixir of life in this beautiful, haunted room, it will never be made.'

'I don't think he did any of his experiments in the house. He used the vaults of the old chapel.'

'But his books would be in the house, no doubt.'

'I am afraid, Miss Powers, that there are none of his books left. I am surprised you did not know they were burnt.'

'Oh yes, of course we knew that. But books get moved, put in trunks, forgotten, borrowed and returned years and years later. There is always a chance that an expert searcher may unearth one, or even a page or two from one. That's better than nothing. Once I found a spill jar full of the most precious pages. My host was just putting a match to one, but the writing caught my eye in time. Haven't you perhaps an old library shelf that's never been touched?'

'I have my own books, but I know quite well what and where they are.'

'Well, somewhere in a dear old place like this there must be a corner where nobody looks. If there is you can trust me to find it. How sweet of you to prepare this lovely tea for me! – if I may suppose myself invited to it? But please be kind and show me the rest of the house first, or else my mind will be wandering.'

'The kettle is boiling,' said her hostess with authority, 'so I think we will have tea first. You shall see the main Norman building afterwards.'

'Thank you so much, you are very kind,' the small careful voice went on. 'I want to see every little corner.' As she spoke she pulled open a door. 'Oh, a staircase. How interesting. And I hope you will show me the vaults.'

'I am afraid I can't do that. Some considerable time ago the remaining walls of the chapel were roofed over. It has been made into a cottage where I have a tenant living. He is a scholar, but not at all the same kind as

Dr Vogel. I would never dream of disturbing him, and in any case even the furnace chimney has gone. Excuse me a moment, Miss Powers, while I fill the teapot.'

As soon as the old lady had gone out, Miss Powers jumped up and opened a little cupboard built into the side of the fireplace. The two boys watched with disapproval, but she turned to them smiling and said – 'A bread oven! Isn't it all interesting! I expect you two know all sorts of special hiding-places? Boys are like water, they seep in everywhere. You probably know things your old lady never guesses? Even secrets from each other, perhaps. Or things you *think* you've kept from each other. But to get his own way everybody needs a moment of power.'

The boys did not answer, from indignation and surprise, but she went on as if nobody expected children to be able to speak.

'I dare say the most valuable books are kept in this Chippendale cupboard. Oh, only sewing materials. I wonder if there is a false back?' She was tapping round the cupboard when Mrs Oldknow came in again.

'What a lovely piece of oak! A family treasure, no doubt. Wood with a surface like that is tempting to the fingers. This carved African head, too. It looks as if it had been polished with caresses.' The last word had unpleasant undertones.

They all sat down at the table for tea. Miss Powers continued her cooing flow of talk, as cultivated in voice as it was impertinent in matter. Usually, talkative people have loud voices from a desire to force people to listen, but this little voice, only just audible, and so very sweet, compelled concentrated listening and pre-

43

vented anyone else from exchanging quieter remarks under cover.

As Tolly and Ping were not included in the conversation but obliged by manners to seem to be following it, they had every opportunity to look long and well at Miss Powers. What first struck Ping was that her face was like a mask. Most living faces show a variation between the right side and the left. Either the smile moves gaily to one side, or an eyebrow tilts, or one ear projects more, or there is only one dimple. The irregularities give vivacity to a face, and as a rule the more the two sides vary the more attractive it is. In Miss Powers's face there was no variation at all. It could have been machine made. Her features were small and regular, her eyes large under heavy lids. A dimple appeared duly on each side of her face when she turned up her smile, as Ping phrased it to himself, though her expression seemed fixed at the point on the dial that said 'Pure and Holy'. An expression that seemed to him too remote to match her pushing behaviour.

Tolly was irritated at seeing his own old lady smothered and wrapped around with a cocoon of softness. He glanced at Ping for an exchange of impressions which would need no more than a look, but as he did so the saintly eyes of Miss Powers narrowed in a sharp side-shot and flickered over them both.

'Do these lucky boys always get a tea like this? How you must spoil them! One can sense that yours is a very happy family. Happy families are not so frequent as people make out. And unfortunately they are easily broken up. Very easily. These small sugared cakes — where do you get them? A present sent from Paris? How opportune! No, no, thank you, no, delicious as

44

they look. I will leave them for the boys. Grown-ups really do better without extra luxuries like that. It is enough for me to look at them.'

In fact it seemed to Tolly that she could not take her eyes off them, that she watched him and Ping eating theirs (which really were very good indeed) till it was embarrassing. About half an hour later when tea was over and they had risen from the table, Mrs Oldknow offered to lead the way upstairs to see the rest of the house. Miss Powers was standing with her back to the table, her hands clasped behind her, lingering to look at the picture over the fireplace, when Tolly, happening to dart back unexpectedly to pick up a pencil that had dropped from his pocket, saw one of the little French cakes move, jerkily, as if a mouse were pulling it. Then it slid over the edge of the plate and twitched its way across the table and into the twiddling fingers held ready for it behind Miss Powers's back. As her hand closed over it and passed it to her pocket, her attention jumped to the picture – a view of Green Knowe in the eighteenth century embroidered with great patience and art in human hair. A sinister work. She studied it with so much concentration that her face went stony hard, and something fluttered in the back of Ping's mind. He was reminded of something but could not think what.

She said nothing, and finally followed her hostess upstairs, slowly, pausing to look at each thing as she went. She might have been preparing for one of those tests when one is shown a tray full of mixed objects for half a minute and then must write down all that was on it.

The house was full of odd things, as always happens when the men of the family have been travellers. Mrs

Oldknow's own collection had been chiefly of pictures, and birds' nests from the garden, but she was a great picker-up of objects that she felt 'belonged' to the house or would add to it. She never bought anything simply because she personally liked it, but only if she felt she was bringing it to its real home. Consequently it was impossible to tell from looking at her possessions what she was like herself.

Before long Miss Powers stopped in front of another picture, this time a Japanese print of a witch casting spells on the sea-shore – an exhilaratingly eerie work of imagination. 'A most rare print,' she murmured, 'most rare and valuable. I wonder how you came by that.'

Mrs Oldknow laughed. 'Someone was here the other day who said, "What uncomfortable pictures you have." But I don't want comfortable pictures. I prefer them to have a nip of otherness, like life. In a house like this there is room for questions as well as answers.'

Miss Powers made a sound like polite laughter, though her look was sharp. 'So you have some answers?'

'Luckily, yes. Some. Enough to be going on with.'

Miss Powers turned to the picture again.

'You two boys!' she said, in a whisper like the sharp rattle of leaves when frightened birds fly out, and startling because till then she had been taking no notice of Tolly and Ping, 'whoever and whatever she is calling will certainly come.'

'She is summoning the wind,' said Mrs Oldknow. 'They are rather wonderful words. Beautiful love-words for a wicked intention:

Come hither, Sir, Come hither my Lord,
Let down your locks so long and flowing.

I like "my Lord", I think of it when there is a stiff
north-westerly gale here. How better could one address
such a force?'

Miss Powers so far forgot herself in surprise that her
clasped hands came apart and hung in the position of a
rook's claws when about to land. Then she folded them
again and keeping her face turned away from the old
lady, said in an undertone: 'You have studied?'

'I wouldn't say so before you. I have no doctor's
degree.'

'So many occult references in the house. A ju-ju
head, a picture in human hair, an incantation to raise
the wind – and here, if I am not mistaken, another of
hypnotic ritual in Bali? Downstairs I saw a dish por-
traying Dagon, the Great Fish God.'

Mrs Oldknow caught the boys' eyes and gave a de-
lighted chuckle. 'All just thrown in as extras,' she said.
'This house is not put out by a few things of that kind.
It has something bigger of its own.'

'Ah!' And Miss Powers backed away murmuring
under her breath what sounded like a string of ancient
names. But Mrs Oldknow was holding open the door
into the Knights' Hall. 'Come in here,' she said, 'and
you will see what I mean.'

Lines of sunshine fell into the room, the longest
coming from the window up under the tent-shaped
ceiling. This was so high that the furniture (of which
there was little except comfortable seating) was
dwarfed to seem a deposit on the floor. Nine-tenths of
the room was empty space, and though Tolly had said
earlier that nothing went on up there, it seemed now to

47

be fully occupied with its own quietness, as if that were something active. Tolly thought the only comparable serenity he knew was that which hung over long empty beaches if you could be the first to get there at sunrise or sundown.

Melanie Powers came through the door and for a split second looked as if she had walked into a trap. Then her two dimples reappeared and she looked around and up.

'Certainly you kept the real surprise till the last. This *is* what I should call an Ancient Monument. Do you have ghosts of Crusaders in here? Funnily enough, not all previous periods of time strike one as old-fashioned. Some seem to come round again quite topically, like persecution, the fall of empires and the inrush of barbarism. But the Crusades are really too old-fashioned to believe in, don't you think? It's all gone. It is meaningless. But of course historically speaking every remnant should be preserved. And of course, too, though the Crusaders, when they weren't scoundrels, were mentally infantile, and the Knights just clanking buffoons, at least King John was real enough. There's always something real about a murderer. I see you have no library. You said so, of course, but I thought that was just your modesty. And something tells me this can't have been the room where Dr Vogel worked.'

'I can show you that if you wish, but it is now the spare room and perfectly up to date.'

'Thank you.' Miss Powers continued looking round, and the boys stood side by side on the stairs leading to their attic. They watched her with the eyes of youth that see what they see and do not try to believe it is something different. They saw their plump affected visitor behaving like an animal that knows there is something just behind, or above or to one side, and cannot place it. Those searching movements of the head were unmistakable.

'These stairs will lead to the boxroom no doubt?'

'They lead to the boys' bedroom, and as they have only just got back from camping and have hardly unpacked I'm sure it is not in a state to be seen.'

'No, it isn't,' said Tolly and Ping together. 'Not at all.'

'Then perhaps next time I may. There must be a fine view from there. There would seem to be a space for possible storage in the apex of the roof above us here?'

'There is,' said Tolly promptly. 'And I have been in it. It has the biggest spiders you ever saw and a ceiling full of smelly bats.'

'Oh dear! You are trying to frighten me. But we must have a look together some time. Spiders have been known to seal books up with their webs, and then cover them over entirely. And some very old books are written on dried bats' wings.'

'They can't be nice books,' said Ping.

Mrs Oldknow smiled quickly at him. 'I don't encourage anyone to go up there,' she said. 'There are no floor-boards and if someone put a foot through the ceiling it's too high to repair without a scaffolding.'

'Anyway, Granny, there's nothing there. I had a torch, I could see.'

'There is something here that might interest you, Miss Powers. You are not perhaps doing justice to the old room, even though I know your first interest is in books. Many things used in building this house were

49

already old when the builders assembled them. Look, for instance, at these stones in the window arch – hold the curtain aside, Ping my dear, so that we can see. Those runes cut in the stone face. They are of course much older than the house. A dedication to powers long forgotten.'

The visitor, politely bending down to look, had her back to her hostess and was taking no notice of Ping. As she recognized these symbols of ancient holy things, a sneer twisted her mask into something lively and real. With a shock Ping recognized her, wondering how he could possibly have failed to do so at first. This was exactly where they had propped the Persian mirror.

She straightened her back. 'These antiquities are quite touching, and I see you take a great pride in them. But wherever these stones were before, there is now not one stone of it left upon another. Otherwise these would not be here. The strength has waned. Don't flatter yourself that your house is invulnerable. However, you said you enjoyed a nip of otherness. I hope your answers hold good. But you would be well-advised to part with *that book* and anything else you have of *those things*. They should be with the proper authorities and properly safeguarded.'

The little voice was sickly and careful, but her listeners could sense a bite of malice and an undershake of anger. 'I must go back now. I have much to do. We shall meet again soon. Please don't bother to show me out. I know my way.'

'Well!' said Mrs Oldknow, when they had watched the unrhythmical feet stamp away up the garden path, 'what do you think of Dr Melanie D. Powers?'

'It's not beetles she's crushing this time,' said Ping, 'it's us. Why did she hate everything so much? She might have been trying to pull the whole place to bits.'

'Perhaps it was only because she couldn't find what she wanted,' Tolly suggested. 'She wanted that book very badly, and I don't believe it was for the Society at all, it was for herself.'

'And it wasn't only that she couldn't find what she wanted. She found something that she didn't like at all.' Ping was remembering the sneer that only he had seen.

'She thought Granny was a witch! Do you remember how she backed away?'

They all three laughed, making up all at once for the politeness imposed on them for the last hour, but in the middle of it Tolly remembered the little Paris cake moving in jerks towards a waiting hand. Would even Ping be able to believe that? Would real witches bother with such petty greediness?

'Did you like her, Granny?'

'I'm sure you know I didn't, I hope it didn't show outside the family. She's a pin-pricker.'

'Do you mean a real one, with wax figures and red-hot needles?'

Mrs Oldknow looked at Tolly, startled. 'I didn't mean that, but I see what you mean. She said a lot of nasty little things, but' – she smiled and tapped her chest – 'I was wearing that Druid's stone and felt very senior.'

'Pin pricker and cupboard opener,' said Tolly, 'mean holy sneak thief.'

The old lady laughed and gave him a push. 'Real schoolboy language,' she said, 'the truth, the whole truth and a lot of triumph beside the truth. My impression was that she went away in a rage. So probably we shan't see any more of her. I didn't really want her as a neighbour.'

'Do you know –' Tolly and Ping began simultaneously, but then they decided to confide in each other first, and went off, Tolly's arm round Ping's shoulder, to compare notes. 'We'll tell you later,' they called back.

The evening light was streaking low across the garden, laying out the shadows of the trees across the lawns. Every west-facing window was a little sun. Mrs Oldknow made a tour of her long rose-beds on the watch for signs of mildew. She saw with the greatest pleasure how every bush held up its crop of buds ready to open in the last big flowering of the year. For many varieties the autumn flowering was the best, and for the old lady, who was quite aware that people do not live for ever, this festival was important. Her roses were her passion. They seemed to her the clearest sign of the essential nature of life. She looked at the sky, at the red sunset that was shepherds' delight, and promised herself joy.

She passed through into the inner garden where the air was dreamy with the scent of heliotrope. Blackbirds, thrushes and robins were singing the sun down. On the moat moorhens were calling their long-legged inexperienced youngsters. They seemed to be saying, Fox, fox, fox, like a lesson to be learnt. The heron flopped slowly across the sky to the north, crossing a flock of rooks returning homeward from the fields. The old lady turned back to the house just as the sun set with a final exchange of flashes between it and the living-room windows. She could hear Tolly and Ping coming along the river path, and smiled at the sound of their voices, which had that comfortable interchange that only best friends have and which cannot be imitated.

They all went in together.

Later that evening in their bedroom, Ping and Tolly were discussing what they had seen in the Persian glass and what it might mean. They regarded the glass with some fear, and yet it was obviously on their side.

'A kind of watchdog that hears and smells before we can,' said Tolly.

'But not very long before,' Ping reminded him. 'Suppose the reflection only lasts as long as the thing lasted. We might not have happened to be looking. A watchdog stops barking as soon as whatever it is has gone. And I suppose the glass has to be facing in the right direction. Where we have put it now, it only reflects our room and part of the meadow. Let's put it nearer the window, facing toward The Firs and the river path.'

They hung the glass against the wall of the window seat, where it reflected all the approaches to the house from that side, and a great deal of the garden and orchard. The trees and hedges were in leaf, so that it was hard to see more of people moving about outside the garden than perhaps a pair of legs beyond the arched base of the hedge, or a brightly coloured hat moving above it. Once inside the boundary anybody would be clearly seen.

Tolly and Ping looked searchingly in the glass. They

were not at all sure they believed in it, but it is always worth trying to see if an exciting idea works. They saw the moon shining on The Firs. It was a desolate-looking house entirely surrounded by high untidy hedges. Anything could go on inside there and nobody would know. The boys could see no difference at all between reflection and reality. They grew tired of looking in the glass where nothing happened, and eventually went to bed.

The head of Ping's bed was against the wall beside the window. As he lay, he could see in the mirror the moon reflected in the river. The moon was bright and the unquiet disc in the water was tiring to watch. To look fixedly at a bright object makes anyone sleepy. Ping dropped off and half woke again with the fascinating square of glass still in view. Now the moon was so high that the trees and shrubs at the end of the garden wore their shadows close round them. At one moment he thought he saw something moving there – something that drew out of the shadows, and went back into them. He propped himself on his elbow to get an easier view. There was nothing, and he lay down to go back into sleep. But whatever it was leapt out of the shadows and ran about the lawn. Sometimes it seemed on all fours and sometimes upright, and it had a whitish face. With much erratic coming and going, stooping and rising, it passed towards the house and out of the mirror. Ping leapt out of bed to wake Tolly. The glass showed nothing but the moonlit garden. 'If it was a dream it was a horrid one,' said Ping, as they got back into bed.

The next morning, not long after breakfast, the boys

and Mrs Oldknow were clustered with their heads together over an open *Book of British Birds,* to see if it was really a firecrest that Ping and Tolly had seen in the orchard. There was a tap on the french window that could have been one of the bluetits, always wanting attention. Tolly looked up casually – and there was Melanie, as he and Ping called her, gazing through with her hand on the knob, already coming in. She seemed rather bigger than he had remembered.

Few things are more annoying than intrusion into one's house from the back without warning. Even intimates seldom do it, and even to them peering through windows is only admissible after every bell and knocker has been tried. Mrs Oldknow clucked in irritation, while the boys stood one at each side of her, Tolly's arm still round her shoulders. 'I hope I am not intruding?' the visitor said in her gentlest voice, smiling like someone who wants to be an old friend. 'At least I see you have no other visitor, I live so near, you know, I thought perhaps I might just pop in. I am afraid I left rather precipitately yesterday afternoon, and it may have seemed curt when you were being so kind. But I have a great deal of work on hand and try to keep exact hours. Certain times for certain things is the rule. But it is just your kindness that made me feel I could dare to come again. How beautiful your garden is! I hardly noticed it yesterday, my eyes were on the house. You must have one or two gardeners all the time; and that helps to keep out trespassers.' Mrs Oldknow did not answer this except to say, 'Do come in.' There was no need to say that Boggis was on his annual holiday.

'Thank you. Of course the riverside with the topiary is the most spectacular, but this inner garden, though less formal, is almost more beautiful, and *quite* private.'

'We like to think so,' said the old lady blandly.

'Nobody at all could see what went on here.'

'No,' Mrs Oldknow smiled at Ping, remembering his dear Hanno. 'There have been unexpected inhabitants before now. Well, what can I do for you, Miss Powers? We can't oblige you with the book you want even if we wished to part with it, because we haven't got it.'

'Oh, forgive me if I pressed too hard. I don't suppose you have any idea of the strength of passion that can be felt over purely professional or academic matters. But you were kind enough to say you would show me the room where Dr Vogel studied, and with my rather hurried exit' (she laughed at the theatrical word she had chosen) 'that was omitted. Dare I ask? Perhaps the boys could show me and then you need not be disturbed.'

'It is no trouble. We will go up now and then you need not lose time from your work. It is a room only used when I have visitors, I doubt if Ping has ever been in it.'

The spare room was an Elizabethan lean-to built against the outside wall of the Knights' Hall, from which a window looked down into it. There was also a new window looking outward on a little courtyard. The room was bright and orderly with no corners where mouldering books could lie unseen.

'This is where Dr Vogel kept his library and where poor little Roger had his lessons. I wish very much we had the globes, but they are, I think, in the Museum. Of course, in those days this was a fixed window with leaded panes. No wonder Roger was ill, cooped up all day without any air. This roof at right angles to us that we are looking down on, is the one over the old vaults which were under the chapel. The walls of the chapel itself have gone. They were called vaults because they were vaulted,' she explained to Tolly, 'but they were not underground.'

'So the chapel was joined on to the house?'

'The walls joined as now. I am sure there must once have been a door into it somewhere on this level connecting it with the house.'

'But there is still,' Miss Powers put in briskly. 'Just here, where you would expect it.'

Behind her Tolly and Ping grinned widely as her hand went out to the door handle. Yet another disappointment awaited her. The door opened into a large closet, fitted with shelves and coat-hangers where coats and dresses in polythene bags hung in a row.

'Would this be a door-post?' she asked, putting her hand on a projecting line of masonry.

'I'm afraid not, it's the kitchen flue,' said Mrs Oldknow patiently, with a flicker at Tolly.

'The chapel ran east and west,' Melanie continued, leaning well out of the window. 'The altar at the far end. Was the base of the altar still there when you roofed it over?'

'I can't tell you. The joists were intact, and on them was a remnant of tiled floor and a lot of rubble. But it had been roofed before my time. I only repaired it and plastered the inside of the vaults to make it habitable.'

'You *plastered* it! But the walls must have had all sorts of graffiti, initials, diagrams, runes. And even symbols painted on them.'

57

'Exactly,' said Mrs Oldknow, with her lips twitching. 'They had.'

Melanie drew in her breath but went on coaxingly, 'It must make a strange little study. Do you think your scholarly tenant would show it to me?'

'I would not like to ask him. You must excuse me, but he came here to work in quiet and I observe the rules absolutely.'

'Doesn't he sometimes go out?'

'Perhaps, but that is not the time when I would go in.'

'Ahaha! No, don't think I could imagine you capable of that. But there must be someone who goes in to clean for him? He is an interesting subject, your scholar. What made him choose this particular corner? For – forgive me – the vaults must be rather rudimentary comfort, even modernized.'

'I think he loves the age and quietness, just as I do. His subject is ninth-century manuscripts.'

Miss Powers jerked back from the window. 'What is his name?' she hardly found voice enough to ask.

'Mr Pope.'

'Not Honorius Pope?'

'No. Maitland Pope.'

'That may not be his real name, of course.'

The old lady's lively wrinkles escaped into contagious merriment. It was as inoffensive as a burst of sun on wind-creased water. 'Of course it's his real name! In the name of honesty and common sense why ever not?' The boys looked at her with affection. They trusted her absolutely. Melanie Powers looked too, the politeness fading off her face for a moment and leaving neither warmth nor respect. Then she laughed too.

'I stand rebuked by country innocence. I dare say I am corrupted by too much travel. For a thing to be what it seems is against all philosophy. Your candid company will be good for me. Yes, indeed. And now I have an idea. An excellent idea. I do hope you will agree. And why not, when it is clearly to everyone's advantage? Since you have one scholar here and obviously have a strong and sympathetic feeling for scholarship, why not let this room to me for my work? It would suit me admirably – so secluded and well-lit. I would live at The Firs and merely come here to work. There is not a single well-lit south-facing room there. A month would probably give me time enough. We might even find Mr Pope and I could collaborate, since our fields overlap. I would pay whatever you suggest. You would only have to give me a key and I would come and go without disturbing you at all. You wouldn't know I was there.'

Tolly thought that was exactly what they wouldn't like, and his face always showed his feelings. Ping's face was grave and polite, but he was thinking that she didn't yet know about the Persian looking-glass.

Mrs Oldknow set their minds at rest. 'I am sorry to disappoint you, Miss Powers, but I couldn't consider it for a minute. I need the room for my guests.'

'Only for a month! Have you anyone coming? No, of course you haven't, confess it. When I want something I am not easily put off.'

'I realize that, but I have no intention at all of sharing my house.'

Miss Powers gave a chuckle that was less like a turtle-dove than a rattle of bones. 'We shall see. There are more ways of entering a house than through the doors.

And now I will disturb you no longer. I will let myself out the way I came.'

'The front entrance is the usual and the shortest way,' said her hostess. 'Tolly, show Miss Powers out that way. So far she has only come through the back. Good-bye, Miss Powers.'

'This way, please,' said Tolly, polite and business-like. But as soon as she was alone with him and facing the staircase into the hall, where already a long mirror reflected the banister rails and their descending legs, the visitor became arch and condescending. She bent down and poked Tolly in the ribs.

'Poker face! I don't like children to be stiff with me. Let's play rabbits. Rabbits always follow the known track. Come on, race me!' Away she went at full speed, back on her tracks through the house, down the other staircase and so out at the back. Tolly was not going to play rabbits with her, and considered himself absolved from seeing her out. Instead, he watched from a window to see that she really went, and there she was going down the garden. He was thinking how silly grown-ups sometimes are. Especially as she was not the little cosy body he had first thought, but quite big.

Tolly went back to the others. 'She wouldn't go down the front stairs. She shied like a pony and knocked me in the ribs and said she wanted to play rabbits,' he said, contemptuous and yet uncomfortable.

'Has she gone?'

'Yes, I watched her as far as the gate.'

'What a relief! She's a very pushing person.'

'Now what would you like to do today? I want to go

to Penny Sokey and I wondered if you would like to take me there by river. We could have a picnic and you could bathe. September is the loveliest time for being on the water. Unless you have any other plan?'

They were all agreed, and an hour later the picnic was ready and the boys had the punt waiting.

While Mrs Oldknow was locking up the house (which she rarely did, but just now Boggis was not there to keep off trespassers) Mr Pope came out from his cottage, in his dressing-gown in which he always worked in the morning. He was a vigorous, practical-looking man with a mixture of humour and reserve in his face that made the boys long to talk to him but not dare to do so.

'I'm glad to see you locking up,' he said. 'I was just coming to tell you that there seems to be someone snooping around. Last night I woke up to see a face pressed to the window near my bed. You can't recognize a face with the nose and mouth pressed in. I couldn't tell if it was man, woman or boy. I got out of bed and leant out and shouted, but I only saw the branches swing back where someone had passed through. I wondered whether you had asked the police to look round. But the police would have answered when I shouted.'

'Thank you for telling me, Mr Pope. Perhaps I should tell the police. But I don't really think they would find anything worse than courting couples.'

'Do you think it could have been a werewolf?' asked Ping casually.

'That would discourage the lovers far more than the police,' she laughed. 'But I am afraid it is too much to hope for, Ping.'

Mr Pope, however, seemed to consider Ping's words. He looked at him with kindly appraisal, but said no more.

It was one of those September days that are like June come again but with a thrilling lightness in air and sky instead of languor. Only here and there had a leaf turned from green to gold. Long threads of gossamer shone silver against the sky as the punt glided along on the blue looking-glass river. The sun was hot and the old lady sat under her parasol, looking to Ping's eyes very august, like the Empress Mother. She gave the reflection of the punt great dignity. Ping stopped paddling to look at it. 'At any rate,' he said meditatively, 'we shan't meet Melanie on the river. Not if she doesn't like looking-glass.'

'What makes you think she doesn't?'

'Well, there is something about the hall she doesn't like. She just won't go down it. She can't be afraid of birds' nests.'

'She could,' said Mrs Oldknow, almost as if talking in her sleep. 'All those little *Te Deums*. I have a feeling they would annoy her. What she calls country innocence. How hot it is! You know, her last words were like a threat. "More ways of getting into a house than through the door." Well, let her try!' She twirled her parasol in irritation. There was a spider dangling in front of her eyes on a long thread from one of the points. She watched it fixedly for a while. Its white belly shone in the sun as it turned. 'It is getting too hot. I wish I had brought a fan as well as my sunshade. Don't you boys feel it?'

'Not specially,' said Tolly.

'It seemed to hit me like a blast. There's no air to

breathe. It gives me pins and needles as anaesthetics do ... Innocence!' She said this last with a voice so unlike her own that the boys looked at her with surprise. The punt moved on in silence for some time between the fidgeting rushes, over water where the occasional fallen leaf floated glued to the surface and the high sky was above and below. The old lady seemed to be dozing. The thin blue lids came down over her rounded eyes and the mischief faded out of her wrinkles. The boys cut out their chatter and paddled quietly and responsibly. Presently as the punt passed under a tall damson tree a thrush dropped a fruit stone which fell on to the taut parasol with a sound like a heavy drop of rain. Mrs Oldknow seemed to force herself to wake. She shook her head angrily and passed her hand over her face. She looked at the boys with unnatural concentration, but could not keep it up. Her eyes closed again and her parasol tipped to one side, trailing its fringe in the water. This was most unlike her usual behaviour. She was not one of those old people who are always dozing off and wake up to talk nonsense. She was always crisp and alert and knew just what she was doing. Tolly leant forward to catch and straighten her sunshade, and felt uneasy. 'Granny!' he said shyly. 'Are you all right?'

'Tolly?' She brought out his name with difficulty. 'Are you there?'

'Of course I'm here. We're in a boat together. Were you dreaming?' As she didn't answer, he went on anxiously, 'Are you ill, Granny?'

She made a great effort. 'Not ill, but I don't feel myself. Isn't that what people say? I feel like someone else. I feel it doesn't matter at all what I do or don't do.

63

Somehow I don't care. I couldn't bother to say no to anything.'

'Can I have a motor-bike?' Tolly asked this as an outrageous experiment, not because he meant to take advantage.

'Yes, of course, have anything you like.'

'Can Ping have one, too?'

'Yes, yes.' Her eyes were closing again, but she fought it off, with that strange fixed look at the boys. 'And it's not because I care for you. I know your names, but it seems I don't care at all what happens to you. Why should I?'

At these dreadful words the bottom fell out of Tolly's world.

She gave a silly wicked laugh that was not hers at all, but both boys had heard it from someone else. It was followed immediately by a deep gasp such as a drowning person might give, and the old lady looked at them with desperate eyes and said indistinctly, 'Somebody's getting at me.'

Ping jumped up, feeling in his trouser pocket, pushed past Tolly and knelt in front of Mrs Oldknow. 'You forgot this,' he said, putting the Stone of Power round her neck and tucking it in under her pullover. 'I saw it on your dressing-table as I came downstairs to come out. I brought it with me to give you.' Her hand came up to feel for it. It worked like an electric shock. She jumped, gasped, blinked, moved herself all over, her colour drained away and slowly came back. She smiled, and was as they had always known her.

'Thank you, Ping, my dear. Just in time! Oh, bless me, that's better! Whatever was it?'

'You said,' Ping reminded her, still kneeling

anxiously by her feet, 'that someone was getting at you.'

'Heavens! Yes. Turn the boat round, boys, and let's get home as quickly as we can and see what's going on there. Oh, what a horrid feeling of loss it has left! I was thinking the most unlikely, hateful things.'

'Did you really mean what you said?' asked Tolly, whose heart had still not found its normal beat.

'Of course she didn't,' Ping comforted Tolly and the old lady simultaneously. 'It was a demon speaking. Didn't you hear it laugh?'

'I don't care to be a vehicle for demons.' She spoke sharply. 'Surely one has some resistance. Come along, boys.' To please her they paddled hard, but a punt is built for dawdling and whether you maintain an effortless movement of the paddles or use every muscle in your back with the utmost push and strain, it makes little difference to the speed. It only made the way home seem longer.

Mrs Oldknow took pity quickly on the red and flustered faces opposite her. 'I mustn't get nervy,' she said. 'Pull in under this bank of willow herb. I'll sit here and enjoy it. You two have a swim. Then you can rest and eat your sandwiches.'

Ping knew the river much better than Tolly did. He knew the gravel pools clean of weeds, and the little weirs under which you could sit with the water dashing round your neck in rough pommelling. They played about with the abandon of two young dogs. Mrs Oldknow listened to their voices that came now from one side, now from another, calling, defying, spluttering and laughing, now above and now emerging from under the water, to an accompaniment of splash and drip. The river lapped and lisped around her, and now and again tapped a tattoo on the ribs of the punt. One of the things she most missed when they were away was the coming and going of young voices, among the best of natural sounds. Round and across her the swallows swooped, checking their twittering for the moment of contact with the surface of the water to pick up a fly, an almost inaudible water-note that was yet essential to the whole.

With dripping hair, screwed-up eyes and zestful teeth the returned bathers ate the sandwiches which Mrs Oldknow brought out of her basket. Her sandwiches were always a pleasant surprise. They never sank to the level of that bread-munch which can be eaten if you are really hungry. Each little polythene package was her offering to their shared pleasure. And now the swallows had the water to themselves while the boys relaxed and felt the sun on their backs.

As they paddled homeward the boys were thoughtful, remembering the disturbing episode on the way out. They stole glances at Mrs Oldknow sitting eagerly upright at the cushioned end. She gave no sign of impatience and yet her silence suggested it. When at last the home stretch of the river came into view and above the bushes the peaked roof of Green Knowe could be seen, she sighed gratefully. The punt was nosed and sidled in against the bank by the garden gate, and Tolly sprang out to tie the rope and help his great-grandmother out, while Ping steadied the boat.

Mrs Oldknow leant over the gate while they collected their things out of the punt. She looked at Green Knowe and the garden as if she were a traveller and might never see this again. 'The blessed place is still there,' she said, 'just as it was. I had such a dreadful feeling of having lost it, of being away somewhere with you two and not having Green Knowe to come back to. It is bliss to walk up the path again. I don't believe a flower has faded since we went out. I shall have a chair in the inner garden and sit there looking at it till I get used to not having lost it.'

Tolly and Ping did not know what all this was about, but they got her chair out of the garden-room and took it through for her to the inner garden. As they turned into it with their privacy unquestioned, there at the far end by the moat, looking both sinister and formidable, Melanie Powers was waiting.

Mrs Oldknow caught her breath, she was seized with trembling, so that she put a hand on Ping's shoulder for support. But as Miss Powers advanced the old lady pulled herself together. 'I might have known!' she said, her creased apple cheeks going scarlet. 'What reason can she have thought up now?' She snorted, 'I am so angry I think I am going to enjoy it.'

Miss Powers came across the lawn with a business-like confident manner. The affected over-sweetness and over-sensibility had been discarded. There was no insinuating smile on her mask-like face, and without it the exact symmetry was grim. Her voice was still and careful, syllable by syllable.

'I found no one at home, and as I had to wait I felt at liberty to explore the garden. You were away longer than I expected,' she added with a hint of arrogance.

'I had no appointment with you as far as I remember.'

'At your age, people do frequently forget. You doubtless have forgotten the deed I mentioned this morning on which you were to be so obliging as to witness my signature.'

'No such thing was mentioned to me.'

Miss Powers, whose eyelids were normally half lowered like a nun's, for once lifted them to uncover the whole irises of her eyes, which were bright with the empty mechanical ferocity of a tiger.

'You forget too much,' she said. 'It is difficult to impress anything on a very old brain. Let us go in and waste no more time. I have the papers with me.'

'What papers?'

'I will show you indoors. Nobody can sign without a table. Go in, please.'

The boys were scandalized by this treatment of 'Grand', but she only smiled and said, 'After you. You are the guest. Come in, boys.'

'There is no need for children. They can stay outside.'

'I never exclude them.' Mrs Oldknow gently pushed them in.

Melanie Powers unrolled a paper which was seen to be folded in two, leaving only space at the bottom for two signatures.

'It is a deed of sale. There is no reason for you to know the exact nature of my business transactions. All I want is for you to witness that I have signed it.' She then signed it herself, keeping one hand on the fold in the paper.

Mrs Oldknow smiled at her – a funny smile which made the cheeks of Ping and Tolly twitch in sympathy. She looked round for her spectacles, taking her time over it and humming happily. 'My glasses seem to have been spirited away.'

'You don't need glasses for signing your name. It is a quite habitual movement,' Melanie said impatiently.

'But I do for reading with.' She had an air of leisure and enjoyment. 'As you say, I am very old and my senses are impaired. But old people, you know, hate to be hustled. We take our own time. Come, Tolly, my dear, lend me your eyes. What does it say here, by my finger?'

'It says, "in the presence of".'

'Why, Miss Powers, you have slipped up! You have signed in the wrong place. It will read that you have witnessed my signature, not I yours.' She began to draw the paper to her, and Melanie Powers's right hand shot out of her pocket to prevent it. Ping's as quickly dived into the same pocket and brought out the spectacles, which he held out to Mrs Oldknow. She, however, was trying to prevent the papers being snatched from her, and clutched them to her body, where Melanie's knuckles, as she pulled, touched against something hard that certainly wasn't the old lady's collar-bone. She let go, staggering slightly, nursing her arm and whistling in and out through her teeth as people do in pain. The old lady quietly adjusted her glasses and spread out the document. It was written in fantastically elaborate writing, the looped and festooned capital letters done in dark red ink.

'Look, boys! Dr Vogel couldn't have done it better. You can hardly object to my reading this to them, Miss Powers, since in fact it concerns them as much as me, and me even more than you.

𝔚𝔯𝔦𝔱𝔱𝔢𝔫 𝔴𝔦𝔱𝔥 𝔞𝔫 𝔲𝔫𝔰𝔲𝔩𝔩𝔦𝔢𝔡 𝔮𝔲𝔦𝔩𝔩 𝔬𝔫 𝔣𝔞𝔦𝔯 𝔭𝔞𝔯𝔠𝔥𝔪𝔢𝔫𝔱 𝔭𝔯𝔢𝔭𝔞𝔯𝔢𝔡 𝔦𝔫 𝔞𝔠𝔠𝔬𝔯𝔡𝔞𝔫𝔠𝔢 𝔴𝔦𝔱𝔥 𝔞𝔫𝔠𝔦𝔢𝔫𝔱 𝔭𝔯𝔞𝔠𝔱𝔦𝔠𝔢.

THIS CONVEYANCE, made the.......... day of...............

19—, The moon being in the third quarter and Mercury and Saturn in harmony, BETWEEN LINNET OLDKNOW widow, of Green Knowe in the county of Huntingdon (hereinafter called 'the Vendor') of the one part, and MELANIE DELIA POWERS of Geneva (hereinafter called 'the Purchaser') of the other part. WITNESSETH that in consideration of the sum of £10,000 paid by the Purchaser to the Vendor (the receipt of which sum the Vendor hereby acknowledges), the Vendor as Beneficial owner HEREBY CONVEYS UNTO THE PURCHASER immediately without any ill will delay noise distortion or evasion ALL THAT MANOR HOUSE building and land containing 7 acres situate at Green Knowe. TO HOLD the same unto the Purchaser in fee simple with all that appertains thereto whether known or hidden visible or invisible quick or dead, active or latent and the powers conjunctive thereto. IN WITNESS whereof the parties hereto have hereunto set their hands and seals the day and year first above written

by the ineffable names of Gog and Magog

SIGNED SEALED AND DELIVERED ....
by the said LINNET OLDKNOW

> Summoned by my will and pleasure in this place and before this circle whereto you shall be bound by the chains of your soul.

In the presence of:

Melanie D. Powers.

I do not know, Miss Powers, if you do all your legal transactions by hypnotism, but everybody has their failures. You have betrayed your method and we have been warned. Here is your document. I have no intention of selling my house to you or anyone else. And I will say good-bye.'

Melanie Powers was unable to speak. She looked as

angry as a circus tiger flexing its paws as it looks at the trainer's electric stick. She made for the door, and there she turned, standing on the step and towering over the old lady. But even now she did not raise her voice, and the words that she said, falling like the slow drip of a tap, were more venomous than mere anger would have been.

'Do you challenge me? A weak old woman and two boys sentimentally loyal for what they can get? You think you are somebody, with your precious house. But I will have what I want.'

There was a silence after she had gone, and then Tolly said:

'Little kid, little kid, let me come in,
    Or else by the hair of my chinny chin chin
    I'll huff and I'll puff till I blow your house in.'

'I'll just go and make sure she goes,' said Ping, and sped off to a front window, where he watched from behind a curtain. Half-way down the path Melanie turned a face of hatred at what she thought was an unseeing house, and as she passed the rose-beds and found herself breathing in their soft blessing of scent, she spat as countrymen do when they smell drains. 'She's gone,' he said when he came back. 'Did she think you would sign it?'

'She thought she had fixed me so that I would. But for Ping's presence of mind in the punt, we might all have been turned out. Who can prove in a court of law that they were hypnotized? We might have disputed the deed on the ground that the wording was mad and therefore the contract null and void. But no one could prove which of us was the mad one. Perhaps I even look

71

the madder of the two. And I would have to be, to sign it. In any case it would have put me to an immense amount of trouble. She might even have used its nuisance value to blackmail me. Now I suppose we must consider ourselves besieged. I wonder what she thinks she can do.'

'I shall bring down the witchball and hang it here near the door,' said Tolly, 'so that she can't keep coming in this way.'

'I see that you and Ping are agreed about her demon. But I haven't seen anything worse than an affected, greedy, false and detestable person. Hypnotism is said not to be particularly difficult, but it is always hateful even when it is not dishonest. If she was going to hypnotize me, she could have done it without trickery. She must have put that in because she can't enjoy anything without it. All these cheats are fundamentally silly.'

'All the same, you said we were besieged.'

Tolly and Ping went up to fetch the witchball. Tolly carried it in his arms while Ping opened doors for him and brought the step-ladder. They hung the ball on a branch of the yew tree in such a position that no one could come to the back of the house without passing it. The yew tree was as tall and wide as the house, its branches were very long and beautifully drooping. The great silvered globe hanging among them six feet up looked as if it belonged to the garden, belonged to the tree. It had a compelling dignity, and the reflection of the house curled lovingly round it.

'There!' said Tolly with pride. 'Now I'll put your chair here and you will be all right.'

'Thank you – that will be perfect. I find that fighting against hypnotism is very tiring, and fighting against rude persons in the flesh more tiring still. It was all too nasty and too fantastic. I shall have a nap, but I shall be quite safe this time.'

'You don't want us for anything else now?'

'No, my dears. Go and sharpen your wits on whatever boys do. I shall need them later, I expect.'

Ping and Tolly left her, safe as they hoped with the Druid's Stone and the witchball. Tolly had an idea to put to Ping.

'That Melanie creature is particularly curious about the roof of the old vaults. I'm sure we could get into it somehow. There must be a way, because Mr Pope's cottage has water pipes and electricity wires that go up through his ceiling. So the workmen must have got in somewhere to do it. Let's go into our spare room and look round.'

They hung out of the spare window to look at the tiles of the cottage. Over the far end sprawled jasmin and a delicate small-leaved rose, and over the near end a mass of Traveller's Joy coming up from the far side where it had first wrapped up St Christopher and then felt for wider support. There was no sign of a skylight, so no entrance that way. The length of the roof was four times as long as the floor of the closet that had interested Melanie Powers, which was in fact contrived in the end of the roof nearest the house.

They soon found that the shelves in it were not fixed to the wall but were complete in a frame which could be pulled out. In the wall behind it, at floor level, was a small square door through which a man could squeeze if he were lightly built. Inside it was quite dark. Tolly was to go in first as the idea had been his, but when he put his head through and one hand, he came up against a substance so unrecognizable as to be frightening. He backed out quickly and shut the door on it.

'It's full of some sort of stuff like – like beards. We need a flashlight.'

When they had found one each, they returned and reopened the door with care. They lay side by side and played the lights on the interior. The whole space between the rafters and the joists was filled with skeins of dry white tendrils which had, when new, threaded between the tiles from outside. They had grown in and out of each other in a kind of wild knitting, looking for light and finding none and struggling with each other, till the space had filled up. Most of the mass was dry and stringy, but the newer threads still had a ghostly sap and a suggestion of feeling about for something.

'However are we going to search that? We can't even get in, and if we did, we couldn't see what was there. I supose it is only that Traveller's Joy stuff that grows over the roof. Having got in, you'd think it would have the sense to feel a way out again, not just go on growing and growing obstinately where it can't. I wonder if anything lives in it.'

'It would be a kind of eiderdown heaven for field-mice. Or perhaps somewhere there's a little corner broken off a tile where a wren could get in.' These were Ping's suggestions and they made Tolly feel better.

'We could cut it all down,' he said, 'but then it would all be lying heaped up on the floor, and I suppose if there was anything here before the stuff began to grow, it would be lying on the floor, not floating in the air.'

74

'It might have got hammocked up in the tangling business.'

'Let's each cut a way through at the bottom. We'll wriggle along across the joists on our stomachs. The stuff we cut down will make a kind of padding under us and help to keep our toes from poking through. There don't seem to be any spiders. And really it smells quite nice, like a hayloft.' They cut and wriggled and cut and wriggled and presently they were both in, out of sight of each other.

'Ugh!' said Tolly suddenly with feeling. 'There's a very dead bat here, all stretched out. No, it isn't. Yes, it is. Ping! It is one of Melanie's bat books. Back out and let's look at it.'

Backing out was harder than going in, because the weight of growth above them tended to drag up their pullovers. They dusted themselves and took Tolly's find to the window. It was nastier in full daylight than he had realized, like an unclean piece of a mummy. The claws were still on the corners, making hooks to hang it up by. It was indeed a bat book. The skin had been cured and dried, the wings stretched to their full extent. The bat's furry back was the leather that joined them. Inside in dim and dirty but slightly phosphorescent white paint there was writing. A bat's wing makes a small sail-shaped page. The first was taken up with these words –

THE LANGUAGE
KNOWN TO US AS
CROSSING THE RIVER

The other side was filled with strange signs, over each of which someone had written in a browning black

75

THE LANGUAGE KNOWN TO US AS CROSSING THE RIVER

that looked like blood much smaller letters now almost invisible.

'It's a witch's code!' said Tolly in triumph. 'No, it's an alphabet. And it goes backward. Look, A is at the end.'

'That can't be what she wants so badly that she will give £10,000 for it. She must know the alphabet by now. I mean, if she is a witch and if she is any good. There must be something else. It could be something stronger than anything she's got. Perhaps she is even afraid of it. *She* said something about the altar. Might not special things be hidden under it? Let's put the bat-book somewhere safe and then go on looking.'

'I know – upstairs behind the Persian Glass.' Tolly ran up to the attic to hide it. He paused while the glass was in his hands to look for any warning it might give before he disappeared again under the cottage roof. Nobody was approaching. He flew downstairs and rejoined Ping for the search. 'What do you suppose we are looking for?' Tolly called to Ping, prone under the hammock haystack. 'I hope it isn't Nose of Turk or Tartar's lips.' He had been doing *Macbeth* at school.

'It might be a necklace of male and female teeth,' Ping suggested, remembering stories told by his Chinese grandmother. 'But *she* said it was a book, if she ever tells the truth. I can see the end wall. We must be near where the altar was. There's a low stone step here. Have you got there, Tolly?'

'Yes, I've found it. There's a shallow pit in the floor.'

From underneath came a low continuous sound not unlike ritual chanting.

'Whatever's that?' asked Ping.

'That's Mr Pope dictating into his tape recorder. He

77

does his books like that. I have often heard him. It's all in Latin. He must wonder what's going on up here.'

There was silence for a while, except for the rustling made by their hands in the straw and the muffled baritone underneath.

'There's an old riding-boot or something here,' said Tolly. 'With a rat's nest in it, judging by the chewed up bits round it. I can't move it. Can you come and help?'

What Tolly had taken for the leg of a riding-boot turned out to be the back of a massive book bound in leather. It was difficult to recognize it because it was swathed round and tied together, not with cobweb but with Traveller's Joy, and this had to be cut away strand by strand. The back was cracked, and had been much eaten by rats. One cover was detached, the corners rounded and ragged. However carefully the boys pulled, bits of pages and whole pages came adrift. The inside, as Tolly had guessed, had been used for a rat's nest. A semicircle as big as half a saucer was missing from most of the pages. These were elaborately decorated in gold and colour and written by hand. Each page was in two columns, a different language in each. The capital letters were combined with pictures of beasts, and the general lettering most beautiful and clear, but for there being no break between one word and the next.

The book was so rotten, broken-backed and fly-away that the boys had the sense to close it and keep it together as much as they could. The title was 'DECEM POTENTIAE MOSIS'.

Mrs Oldknow, waking after a delicious nap, saw

Ping peering out of the living-room door. His hair was blond with straw dust and his clothes almost as bad.

'Are you alone?' he whispered.

'Why, yes,' she answered, catching his excitement and looking all round. 'What is it?'

'*Tolly's found it*. Could you come in? We daren't bring it out.'

'Yes, of course. Pull me up, Ping darling. My leg is still asleep. There we are. Thank you. I am agog with curiosity.' On the table indoors was lying *Decem Potentiae Mosis* covered over with a cloth 'in case Melanie should look through the window'. When Mrs Oldknow saw it, she was as impressed as they could possibly have wished. They explained where they had found it, in the floor under the place of the altar.

'We were as careful as we could possibly be, but it's all dropping to bits. How old do you think it is? Do you think it is older than printing, or written like this because it is secret? Is it all in Latin?'

The boys poured out questions, while Mrs Oldknow said nothing but Good gracious! or Bless my soul! At last she came round from her surprise enough to say, 'We must take it to Mr Pope. He'll know what it is and what we should do. Will you carry it, boys?'

They went out at the side of the house across Mr Pope's private little courtyard (where once, long ago, Dr Vogel had his bonfire of books) and Mrs Oldknow knocked at the door.

'Who's there?' he answered impatiently, and they heard his chair pushed back from the table.

'It is I, Mrs Oldknow.'

In a minute the door was opened and he stood there

smiling, but looking as if the interruption couldn't be too short.

'I hope you'll forgive us, Mr Pope, when I show you what we have brought. Will you look at this and tell us what we ought to do with it? The boys have just found it. Exactly over your head, as it happens.'

Mr Pope looked at it and whistled his astonishment at its existence and his sorrow at the worn corners. He opened the book, which he caressed as if soothing something alive, with such reverent and expert handling that the boys blushed for their best care, seen now to have been only moderated violence. His fingers seemed to have a special sense for the mastery of rotting parchment, and a foreknowledge of crumbling or cracking leather. When he saw the rat-eaten pages he swore, touching in imagination what was gone. At the end of the book were several pages that were stained but quite whole. He stopped to read these, forgetting his company and his face grew brilliantly happy as if he were drinking champagne.

'It is the most extraordinary piece of luck that ever came my way. And exactly at the right moment too. Mrs Oldknow, thank you for bringing it for me to see. I want time of course to examine it, but you can see it is a translation into Latin from Hebrew. Written in Spain in the ninth century, I'm almost sure. The binding can't be original. That would probably have been of wood. It was a famous book, of which there was thought to be no surviving copy. This therefore must be unique and of the very greatest value.'

'What sort of book is it?'

He laughed. 'It's a book of magic, pre-dating the *Key of Solomon*. The Ten Powers of Moses – presumably what he practised on Pharaoh. We are seldom reminded that Moses was a great magician. Where it touches on my work is that I have noticed that early Celtic legal documents seem to be stiffened, or laced, as you might say, with traditional magico-religious phrases or allusions. This book will probably give me the original formulae, and show me others I have missed. One piece of a page the size of my hand would have been of value, if the book itself had never been found. You two boys, considering that you were larking around and had no knowledge of what this was, were not, as boys go, too desperately damaging. Were there bits of this lying about – loose pages, or even scraps big enough for a few characters to be written on them? You see, we could try each bit against the torn edges and perhaps get another word or even finish a sentence.'

'Yes, sir,' said Tolly. 'There are lots of tiny pieces pulled off by rats. But you don't know what it is like in there. They will be awfully hard to collect.'

'Mrs Oldknow, may I go with the boys and see where it was found?'

'Yes, certainly. Make them pick up every precious bit.'

'Then let us go at once. I'll take this box to collect the pieces in.' He was crossing the courtyard, in his eagerness leaving the door of his room open.

'Please, sir,' said Ping, 'you remember that face you saw in the window? That is someone who wants to steal the book. Shouldn't you lock it up?'

'You are quite right, of course. And I must put it out of sight. Mrs Oldknow, the book is really too valuable to keep in a private house. You should insure it. And even so it should be in a safer place.'

'That's what Melanie said,' Tolly commented in surprise.

'Melanie?'

'She's the other one who wants to have it.'

Mr Pope positively blushed. 'I don't feel I'm quite guilty of that,' he said to Mrs Oldknow. 'But I admit that it would be a great privilege to be allowed first go at it. Who is my rival?'

'Melanie Powers, Doctor of Philosophy, of Geneva and Jerusalem. Do you know her?'

'I never heard of her. She can't be in my line of country.'

'She says she is looking for rare books known once to have been in famous seventeenth-century libraries, on which she is compiling a book. She is quite unscrupulous, otherwise it would seem foolish to get into a panic about something that has lain safely in the house since at least 1630.'

'Perhaps I should take it straight to the Museum library,' he said unwillingly, 'where it can be safely locked up. I can go and work on it there every day.'

'So could Miss Powers. She would only have to ask for it.'

'Of course. That wouldn't do at all. Some people don't scruple to take away pages, and from a damaged book like this it would be too easy.'

'Would you consider working in the spare room in my house and keeping the book there? At least no one outside could look through the window, and there would be four of us on the look out. Your cottage is particularly vulnerable. We have never had to consider the possibility of burglars here. You'll find the spare room light and good for working in. In fact, Miss

Powers wanted to rent it herself. She seemed to have a sort of magnetic reaction to the whereabouts of the book.'

'That is probably the best idea, at any rate till I have pieced the thing together, if you will give me that privilege. Then you could send it to an expert manuscript repairer. There is an excellent one in Wales. I would be delighted to take it there myself, if you wished. There are some manuscripts there now that I want to look at. Come along then, boys – show me the way.'

Mrs Oldknow, bending, torch in hand, saw the three pairs of feet disappear under the eiderdown of Traveller's Joy, and then withdrew, very thoughtful, into the garden.

At this time of year the bird population was at its greatest, for there were not only the regular winter and summer residents, but each pair had raised at least two broods during the summer, and the play and chatter of young birds was another of the special pleasures of Green Knowe. People tend to think of young birds as fledglings, foolish, open-mouthed and vulnerable. But there is a happy period when they have learnt to fly and have nothing to do but amuse themselves, which they do with the fantasy, the enjoyable waste of energy and bursts of high spirits, the chasing and shouting natural to any other young creature. Their love of life restored the old lady's confidence and good humour.

She ended her ramble with a sheaf of tobacco flowers and Michaelmas daisies across her arm, and paused near the gate to look at the church clock. The day was fading and she failed to see the dial clearly. She turned her head at the sound of footsteps. Melanie Powers was coming along with a big basket. She passed the gate, but stopped to look over the wall and said, 'Lovely now, isn't it?' in the standard voice of a civil passer-by. 'I can see your heart is in your garden. I'm sure you literally think the world of it. It must have taken you a lifetime to make. If you lost it, you'd never make another. We don't have a second time, do we? I am a botanist myself, but of another kind. I collect the rarer night-blooming wild flowers. An early moon in an opal sky is just the best light for seeing them. The sunlight blinds you to them, you know. Good evening, Mrs Oldknow.'

'Good evening to you,' said the old lady, in a rather schoolboyish voice. But Melanie had passed on, going towards the churchyard.

By the time Mrs Oldknow had put the flowers in water Ping and Tolly were there washing themselves and brushing each other, and full of talk.

'Helping Mr Pope was great fun. He was rather strict and swore at us if we tore anything, but we liked it because he was deadly keen. He minded as much as a dog does. We found a lot of small pieces, and two pages. I asked him what was written on one. He said, "It's a spell. You can try if you like. *Ad daemonem diminuendum*. For the diminishing of a demon." It was:

> "Shabriri
> briri
> riri
> iri
> ri."

As he read it out to us, there was a sound like something sliding down the wall outside. It was horrid. But Mr Pope took no notice so we thought we'd better not. So I said that Shabriri business seemed just silly kid's stuff. He said it was not something to go round chanting just to clear the air. It would only apply to a particular high-up demon. And only because it was his true secret name. He said secret names were the essence of magic. He says he will sit up all night reading the *Ten Powers*. We asked him why he thought Melanie wanted it, if she wasn't interested in his sort of scholarship. He said, I think, something like, "She may be one of those occultists that swarm in women's colleges." Then he said he supposed they would think the source was more powerful than the derivatives, whatever that means. He doesn't talk to us as if we were kids. In fact I think he's really talking to himself.'

'If everybody talked aloud to themselves,' said Ping, 'it would be very interesting. Melanie does it a lot, more than she would if she were wise. Perhaps when people are desperately keen, they can't help themselves.'

'She has just been talking to me over the garden wall, as if nothing had happened. We might have been meeting for the first time. She was going to gather night flowers. I suppose there must be such things. There are a few garden flowers that open at sundown, and I think I've heard of moon flowers in jungles.'

Since the appearance of the flattened face at Mr Pope's window, the boys found that they disliked the idea of the garden at night. This feeling was new to them and they resented it. The whole of Green Knowe, inside and out, had been their own to come and go in as they wished at any hour of day or night. Tolly had had his moments of fear in it when he was younger, but now felt that he had established his right to be there. And had not Ping shared the thicket at night with a live gorilla? Nevertheless neither of them proposed anything that would take them out of doors into the moonlight, beautiful and fairylike though it was. There might, in tropical forests, be satin-white moon-flowers opening, but there might also be climbers with hanging tendrils like nooses that closed round you and squeezed you and sucked your blood. In fact there might be anything anywhere just as horrible as you could imagine it.

They had shown Mrs Oldknow the bat book, holding it out hanging by its claw hook to a pencil.

'Melanie said there might be some. She said it to frighten us, and it does rather.'

'Put it in the fire,' said Mrs Oldknow quickly. But it was summer and there was no fire. She sighed. 'I suppose we ought to take it to the Folk Museum. They specialize in witches' things. It's a nasty object. But ever since that woman came the place is besieged by nastiness.'

Ping carried it upstairs still hanging on the pencil, and transferred it to a nail on the attic wall.

'I hope nothing comes in the night to get it,' said Tolly. 'We haven't got the witchball now. We had better shut the windows.'

'Yes,' Ping agreed. 'But I don't see why anything should come to get it. It could fly away itself. It's got wings. And if even a cake can be made to move —'

'I don't want it flapping about in here all night trying to get out!' Tolly protested. 'I can't bear the idea. But all the same, we don't want to lose it. It's one of the things we've got that she hasn't. Or at least she doesn't know we have. Let's put it in a drawer and shut it in.'

By unspoken agreement they put it in the heaviest bottom drawer, which was empty. Then they sat down on the window-seat to study the Persian glass and compare what it reflected with what they could see for themselves.

Leaning out of the window on their elbows they saw the moon-shadow of the gable lying across the lawn like a tall sail. It amused Tolly to think that they were there in the very top of it. The moon was waning but very bright. The river glinted between the trees at the end of the garden and spread out broad and silver beside the churchyard whither Melanie had gone. The fields were wide, dim and empty as far as one could see. Nothing moved. This huge emptiness made Tolly feel anxiously that there must be something. And in fact, looking at the moonlit tiles, dark walls and white-of-eye window-panes of The Firs, he had a strong impression that it was not as empty as it ought to be. He referred to the glass to see if anything there confirmed the idea, but in the image the only difference was a column of ghostly smoke rising from the far garden. The column thickened and broke up into puffs which exploded, changing shape as they flew, with a rhythm like candle flames that reach out and retract again. Evidently Melanie when she came back was going to make a midnight bonfire. But everything she did was potty.

And now in the real view Ping saw her returning

from her botanical excursion. At first it was just a dark head and shoulders moving along above the wall, but as she reached the gate they saw her clearly enough. She stopped and looked up at the window where they huddled in the dark. The moon would be shining straight into those cold tiger eyes, and perhaps she would not see them. But from the chest of drawers behind them came a thud and flutter such as large moths make. The boys froze in horror, but were distracted by another sound from outside – a muffled howl from the direction of The Firs, and then the clamour of boys in flight. Melanie turned towards her house, and Ping, describing it later, insisted that she *barked*. Then she ran for home with the ease of one used to loping along for miles. You would never have guessed from the irregular way she walked, that she could run like that. She disappeared within the high enclosing hedges of The Firs, and in a moment lights came on one after another, upstairs and down as if a search were being made. At last all was dark and quiet again. Not even the moon glittered in the window-panes. It was too high overhead. A midnight bonfire seemed harmless enough. The boys got willingly into their beds, and after some sleepy guesswork about what was going on, grew warm and comfortable and forgot.

Mrs Oldknow was up very early. She had not been able to sleep because she had had nightmares about hypnotism. Every time she dropped off, she dreamed she was in the boat again and that the enticement of sleep was a trap into which she must not fall. As soon as the sun was up she rose and dressed, and as it was far too early for breakfast she went out to enjoy the noises of the waking garden. At this time of morning, the light breeze should be making the bushes rustle as they shake out their creases and hang their leaves in the sun. The birds take their baths busily in the shallows with much splashing, and those that have bathed already make brisk self-congratulatory sounds as they fluff and preen. The sun was just warm enough to be felt gratefully on the back of the old lady's neck and the dew was steaming. It promised to be another perfect day. But disappointingly this morning the garden seemed at first empty of birds, except for a swarm of long-tailed tits, drooping and rising in flight with musical staccato whistles, which crossed the length of the garden and disappeared beyond. Then she noticed a number of great tits on her rose bushes, where those buds she had admired two days ago were now all ready for the morning's sun to open them out. What were the birds finding there? She sauntered over to look, and was very displeased to see some repulsive maggots boring into the rose buds. These particular pests were new to her. They were puffy, squirmy and white with detestable knowing eyes. The tits were fluttering enthusiastically from twig to twig picking them off.

Mrs Oldknow noticed that a greater number of birds were similarly at work in that part of the garden that lay between the rose-beds and the meadow, beyond which again stood The Firs. As she walked in that direction she was dismayed to see that there was a real plague of these creatures, getting thicker the farther she went. At first she had had to look for them, but soon she saw them everywhere. The bushes were heavy with blackbirds, thrushes, robins and the rest, all eating them as fast as they could. The procession of fumbling, inch-long creatures was finding a devious way through the hedge that bounded the garden. In the field beyond, the advancing army stretched in a moving line all the way to The Firs. The things were approaching steadily in that loathsome motion of pull-out-thin, pull-up-fat. They went up grass stalks and wavered at the top, sure of their direction but of nothing else. They squirmed over the backs of each other, found their way up fallen logs and down the other side. The appalling mass slowly, faintly heaved. When Mrs Oldknow conquered her disgust so far as to bend down to look, she could hear a very soft rubbing and rustling from their bodies against each other. But when she stood she could hear nothing but the birds. She would not have thought there could be so many or so many different voices. They were all there – countless rooks with their still noisier young, moorhens running up from the river afraid all would be gone before they arrived, wild duck more cautiously following the moorhens. Even the swans heavily clambered up the bank and shovelled up the wriggling porridge with their ridged beaks. Now and again they stopped to stretch and clap their wings, and then all the other birds flew up in the air, to return in a moment. Here and there a green woodpecker squatted to eat, shooting out its long sticky tongue. The young magpie family with flashing royal blue wing feathers were hysterical with excitement. A pair of pheasants blazing in the sun, a covey of partridges, all were eating as fast as they could. There was even a family of hedgehogs, eight in all, making this their supper, though blinking and screwing up their eyes in the sun. While the old lady stood there unnoticed in the babel, a heron glided down, dropping its long legs to land as it came. It moved about with long, noble strides, picking out the largest maggots which smaller birds had passed over. And finally, when it seemed the feast was too great for even this number, allies beyond hope arrived in a whirring cloud of starlings, hundreds and hundreds, on their way out to the fields from their sleeping quarters. They settled squawking with glee and hunger, and began as they always do to scatter the meal about, apparently from sheer love of waste and for the pleasure of feeling greedier. In this way many maggots were tossed into the river, where fish rose and gobbled them. The starling backs waddled this way and that, and when they finally took off there seemed not a maggot left.

Mrs Oldknow walked across the field looking carefully. At the other side she met an old farmer as surprised as herself.

'They keep telling us on the B.B.C. as how we shouldn't kill the birds. I reckon we've just had a good object lesson. I wouldn't welcome those things in my fields, that I wouldn't. What's Miss Powers been doing in her garden to hatch out them things? Here's another on 'em.' He picked a survivor up, which Mrs Oldknow felt she never could have done, and chucked it into the river. 'You'd have had no garden left if they'd settled on it overnight. I was going round this side of her hedge late last night setting rabbit snares. It's just the place for them to be lying. And I said to myself then, "What's Miss Powers got dead in there? It smells awful." '

The birds had by now all flown off, except a few

moorhens searching for stragglers. The garden song-sters had returned to their favourite trees. The merry business of the delayed morning bath was taking place with more than usual vigour.

'That was a win on the home ground,' the old lady said to herself as she looked happily round.

Tolly and Ping meanwhile had slept late, tired with so much night watching. When at last they came down, Mrs Oldknow had breakfast ready for them and all the latest news. She told them about the plague of maggots.

'Do you think there will be nine more plagues?' asked Tolly. 'Perhaps she hasn't as many powers as Moses. Did Moses have maggots?'

'Lice, I believe, and locusts. They would have the same effect. But I had some more news from the milk-man. Miss Powers's house was broken into last night while she was out.'

Tolly's and Ping's spoons stopped half-way to their mouths and their eyes came up to hers.

'The neighbours think it was boys from the village, but something seems to have frightened them. They can't have done much, because she hasn't sent for the police. They say she had made herself very unpopular – chiefly because of a dog. She was snooping round the hedges of a cottage some nights ago, and the dog very properly ran out yapping at her ankles. The story is that she spat at the dog, and that it died. I don't like her, but I don't think university ladies know how to spit.'

'She does,' said Ping. 'She spat on your roses.'

'Oh, well,' said Mrs Oldknow, as she poured the coffee, 'she forgot the birds.'

*

After breakfast, the boys, feeling their courage in good condition, went upstairs to deal with the question of the bat book. They opened the drawer with anxiety, and sure enough the bat book had moved. It was hanging by its hook on the front edge of the drawer. They pushed it off and it fell to the bottom as inert as any other dead thing.

'I'm not having this,' said Tolly, with the determination of disgust. 'After all, *it's dead*. I'm going to nail it to the bottom. Watch it, Ping.' He went to fetch a hammer and nails, and the bat book was a dead bat and Ping could see that it was so. He knelt by the drawer and gingerly opened the wings.

'Nail it open,' he said to Tolly, 'then we can learn it, it might be useful.'

With four tacks on each side it was fixed.

'After all,' repeated Tolly, as he tapped them home, 'it is dead.'

But nailed open it looked trapped. They conquered their dislike and settled down to learn the alphabet. That done, they kicked the drawer shut and ran down with relief and off into the orchard, which was the best place for bird-watching. Birds would be a nice change. Mrs Oldknow meanwhile went into the garden to go over the roses again and make sure they were all right.

She found four flowers that the maggots had penetrated before the birds got to work. The heads were hanging down discoloured and swollen. She cut them off, dropping them into a basket where they gave off a bad smell. She threw them on the bonfire, poured paraffin over them and burned them. Then she went back to a garden that was responding to the gentle but potent sun warmth. The roses opened willingly as the dew evaporated out of them. As soon as they opened, the scent spread around them so pervadingly that the flight of the birds fanned it to her.

She walked among them in very great contentment. If she herself was old, the sun was not, and the earth would do these wonders for him again and again.

A passing neighbour called to her over the wall, 'Your roses have never been better, Mrs Oldknow. They really are divine.'

Not a bad word for them, she thought, smiling to herself. The word Rose has lost its old meaning. Now it only means something glossy, that you have, along with cars, washing machines and lovely plastic table-tops. It's only a status symbol. But the old-fashioned roses have always been a symbol for love, and like all ecstatic things they die and come again. And the flower is simply a cup for the scent and the scent is an offering. But these thoughts she kept to herself.

'You know, we all enjoy your roses,' the amiable neighbour went on. 'Yours is one of the few gardens that doesn't make people malicious.'

As she spoke, Miss Powers passed behind her, going in the opposite direction. She had a fixed scowl and did not even say good morning. When she was out of ear-shot, the gossip went on – 'That Miss Powers is getting herself very unpopular in the village. Too full of her-self. And nosey. People don't like nosiness even when it comes from good nature. But if a person hasn't a smile or a friendly word, what are they doing looking in at windows at night? She's a real snooper. She's your neighbour, of course. I expect she has a keen look round every time she goes past.'

'I expect she does.' *

Two hours later Tolly and Ping came back to the house. They had been lying in the orchard munching apples and watching the birds and the field-mice, and laughing at the slow heaving of the ground where the mole was burrowing. They had lain sprawled and content in this most happy and leisurely place, sun-warmed and grass-tickled, and full of talk that was only an excuse for chuckles. In their paradise they were suddenly aware of something wrong. Among all the rustling leafy sounds was one that was too rhythmic, an almost inaudible repeating swish. They sat up to listen. Out of the rushes projected the tip of a tail that twitched with a regular beat. At the water's edge, flat on its belly and ready to strike, a huge black cat lay waiting for an unsuspecting young moorhen, that clucked and flaunted its pretty white tail as it enjoyed the morning. The boys leapt up to intercept the murder.

Now as they came near, they called out to Mrs Old-know. 'There were *two* terribly big black cats stalking the moorhens. We chased them off, but they were very fierce and bold, and wouldn't really go. In fact I thought they would go for us. Anyway, we gave the moorhens plenty of warning. Oh, bother! There they are again.'

Ping shot off like a terrier, into the bushes where the sedge-warblers had nested. Four cats bounded out and went off in all directions. Tolly and Ping shouted in imitations of ruffians with a pack of dogs and charged round the garden after them. All the birds flew up. The air was full of their alarm calls. But cats slip through chinks that seem impossibly narrow, and under the impossibly low. They alter their bodies into any shape they need, and once they have taken cover, they change direction and disappear. The boys were hot and out of breath when they came back.

'Can we go and swim now? If we go upstream opposite the water gates, we can keep an eye on what Melanie is doing as we go past. I don't mean go inside. But we could look through the hedge. After all she does it here.'

On the way out, as they walked along the river bank, they saw a cat with a bird in its mouth, streaking across the field. 'Oh curse! It's got one. I bet they are Melanie's cats.'

They had the river to themselves. The surface was faintly steamy, the current slow. Water is the only element that humans can caress and love as they move in it, as birds do in the air, as horses do on downland turf, with every sense at once, even hearing. For sounds are different when heard over water, or tree-tops, or bare hill-sides. They reach us with all the quality of the place absorbed into them.

The bathe lasted over an hour, including much lying on the bank in the sun, getting up enough energy for another bout. Then hunger seized them and they set out for home.

They walked silently along beside the hedge of The Firs. Through the gaps they could just see that she was there, busy about something, with her back to them, looking very tall. That was perhaps because they were crouching down and the path was lower than the garden. They crept to the gate to see.

She had tied a washing line waist-high between two trees opposite the gate and on this she was pegging up dead birds by the tail. They hung head down with their wings fallen open, chaffie with his crest fallen down too, the known and loved song-birds, Mrs Oldknow's darlings, enough already to thin out much of the joy of the garden. Underneath the line a sleek and sinuous cat reached up, boxing the dangling corpses. Tolly's throat gave out a cry in spite of himself.

Melanie looked up without any change in her expression. She went to the other side of the line and continued her work facing them. She pegged up a robin.

'Thieves,' she said, in her little clipped voice, 'and interfering little nuisances. I don't like interference.'

The boys rushed home choking with rage. As they went in at the gate a cat slipped out between their legs with a great tit screeching in its mouth, and galloped down the tow-path. Another was sitting watching a trimmed yew bush, its eyes fixed on the small tunnel through which the wren habitually went in and out. When Tolly dashed at it, the cat arched its back into a hairpin and spat and lashed out at his bare leg with its claws. Ping seized it by its tail, upright and crooked like a walking-stick, but the cat wound round his arm like an octopus, and he was bitten and clawed. As they went along, cats broke cover, or streaked round corners or simply sat on outhouse roofs looking down on them with unmoving green eyes.

They found Mrs Oldknow tired and distracted.

'It's hopeless,' she said. 'I can keep the birds warned, though now they are all in a panic anyway. But they must come down to feed some time, and that's when they are caught – from behind while they are tugging at a worm. Birds are like peasants, they won't leave their own place whatever the calamity. And these are not stray cats. Not even courting cats. Certainly not cat-

97

lovers' cats. They are as wild and sneaky as they can be. It is the birds they have come for. I suppose we all three think the same thing.'

'It's the second plague,' said Tolly. 'Who would have thought when she first came to tea, all sweet and holy, that she was as bad as that?'

'I seem to remember that we all did,' said Mrs Oldknow. 'She asked me, over the wall this morning as I chased a cat out, if I was reconsidering her proposal. I told her I had never thought about it again.'

The boys did not tell her what they had seen in Melanie's garden, because she was unhappy enough already.

'I thought,' the old lady continued, 'that if we each had a long stick, and had our lunch outside at a stick's length from each other, we could put bird food in the middle and keep the cats off.'

'Oh dear,' she said, when they were stationed in battle order, 'I have never in my life hit anything with a stick. I hope I can hit hard enough.' In fact, she hit as hard as anybody, and with precision.

It was a disturbed meal. Neither they nor the birds had much to eat, though all had some. None had the good digestion that follows a meal eaten in peace.

Mrs Oldknow was tired. She left the boys on guard while she went indoors to rest. They needed to patrol the garden incessantly, disturbing the enemy, which were legion, and so preventing ambush. Even so, in so large an area, with shrubberies where only birds and cats could enter, they could not prevent some slaughter. Every bird that was caught filled their ears with its cries.

By the end of the day the boys were worn out and despairing. This could not go on, and night is the best hunting time for cats. Many were already established in the trees. Sundown was full of agitated cries from birds with nowhere to settle down for sleep. No evening song was heard in all the garden, but tired and frightened plaints and weary wing beats.

Supper was eaten in utter discouragement. The boys could not bear to see 'Grand' so sorrowful. This time Melanie had won a cruel victory. 'One of the cats seemed to me almost as long as a leopard. It was lying along a branch of the yew tree.'

At the word leopard, a thought never very far distant came into Ping's mind, and with it a hope.

'I've got an idea, Tolly,' he said. 'Don't come, please. I'd rather do it alone.'

Neither Mrs Oldknow nor Tolly had the least notion of what was in his mind. He went up to the attic and busied himself there with a fine paint brush, a bottle of black ink and a ribbon of paper. It was important that it should be excellently done, and he spent some time on it. Then he took two of his treasures, the prayer bell that he had brought long ago from a ruined jungle temple, and an envelope containing some of the long black hair of Hanno the gorilla, which the keeper had given him as a keepsake. He put a pair of scissors in his pocket and went downstairs, hoping no one would see what he was going to do.

It was late dusk in the garden, moonless, and from all the darker places green eyes shone unblinking. In the house the candles were lit on the supper table, giving the medieval room a warm, living glow. Ping from outside could see Tolly and his great-grandmother sitting there with nothing to say. If they saw him, it was only as a shadow among shadows.

He made his way to the tree from whose branches Hanno had once leapt down to rescue him. On the spot where his splendid friend had been shot, Ping dug a hole. In this he laid the long black hair, and with the scissors cut off some of his own that fell to mix with it, and tears fell too without his intention because he had loved Hanno more than he could understand. He brushed the earth over it, hung the prayer bell on the tree, and said his prayer in his boy lover's voice, 'O Hanno, come just once again,' then, leaving the prayer bell fluttering a tongue of paper that waved in the dark the one word HANNO, he went away.

To Ping, memories of that great man-animal always filled the garden, and now they were so vivid that he quite forgot the cats and was mooning around alone with his thoughts re-living that time, reluctant to go indoors. He was leaning over the wall looking at the river without seeing it. He did not know how long he had been standing there when there arose from the inner garden such a spitting and screeching of cats as never was heard at any witches' Sabbath. Dark forms fled past him through the hedge and over the wall. He could imagine he even saw the sparks flying from their fur.

Deep quiet followed. Not even that chuckling grunt that Ping would have so loved to hear. Only a few notes of midnight-and-all's-well from a blackbird.

Ping smiled, and went indoors, and could not stop smiling though very weary.

'Ping darling, you have been *ages*. What did you do?'

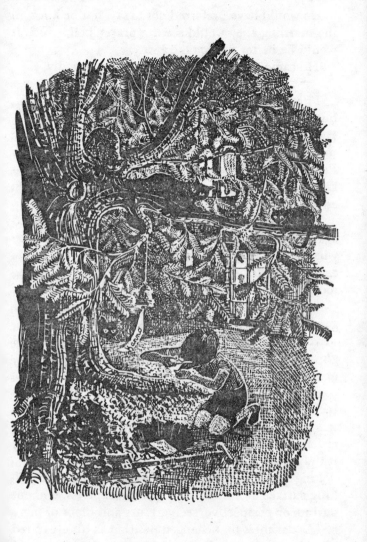

He would have preferred not to say, but he knew in the morning they would see the prayer bell, which it would be better not to take away.

'He came when I called him,' he said proudly.

Three very exhausted people went to bed that night, but as Ping and Tolly passed through the Knights' Hall on their way up, they saw the light burning in the spare room where Mr Pope was at work on the *Ten Powers of Moses*. It was comforting that someone was keeping watch, for they felt they would sleep through anything.

Tolly did in fact go off at once and never moved again all night, but Ping had been deeply disturbed by what he had done, and his sleep was fitful. Once in the early hours he got out of bed to look out. The ageing moon, lying on its back, was rising from a bank of cloud in the east, where was no promise of dawn. The garden had no scent but of darkness and sleep. Ping shivered. He looked in the mirror. In that square of glass the obscure quicksilver showed a sinister picture of the dead moon usurping the place of the sun. The darkness was full of the stirrings that come when power is challenged, as if the upshot could be uncertain. This was a time when any evil thing might gamble on the order of the universe not being stable, and try to swing it to further private ends.

Ping's eyes were heavy but he peered into the baffling surface at a night view grown shapeless, without outline or perspective, seeing blurs and blobs of more or less darkness that changed position as his eyes tired of such acute expanding and focusing. And it seemed that a blackness moved through the shadows, that he could almost be sure it reached and entered the orchard, stayed there a while, and then went back the way it came. Ping's head fell forward on to the glass. He must sleep.

I'll look in the morning, he thought, as he rolled himself up in bed. Does she never rest?

'What next?' said Tolly, as he and Ping ate a large breakfast to fortify them for whatever was coming. 'I bet Melanie is wild this morning. I wonder what she will think up.'

'In all traditional stories about trials of power,' said Mrs Oldknow, 'there are quite strict rules. It is rather like chess. If a piece is taken it can't be used again. You try then to take the piece that took it. Against maggots, birds. Against birds, cats. Against cats, Hanno. Surely, Ping my dear, that must be final.'

'Unless her demon is a very big one.'

'Oh!' said Ping, jumping up, 'we forgot to go and see what she was doing in the orchard last night. She didn't seem afraid of Hanno. But I expect when he had done his job he went back to sleep in his ghost nest. Come on, Tolly.'

They ran off, but very soon were back again.

'We want our gumboots,' they called to Mrs Oldknow. 'We've just seen a snake. It was brilliant buttercup yellow with zigzags down its back. It crossed the big lawn coming straight for us, and looking at us all the time. It passed a few inches from us and went into the long grass. It wasn't at all scared of us.'

'There have always been occasional adders in the wild part,' said Mrs Oldknow. 'Perhaps they are descended from Dr Vogel's pets! With your gumboots you will be all right. Just be careful you don't put your hand on one by mistake. There can't be many. I haven't seen one for years.'

The boys set off again, avoiding the long grass till they came to the orchard where all the grass was long.

The orchard was their favourite part of the garden and almost the wildest. It had a long hedge of nut trees where the squirrels played charmingly. Apples and pears could be picked as you walked. A ladder was left against the big pear tree for this purpose. Along the banks of the moat plants of many kinds that had no right in an orchard at all grew riotously. The leaves were now beginning to turn, the cherry to vermilion and the pear to crimson. Loosened leaves took off like butterflies and red admirals lay open on logs like fallen leaves. There were birds enough, and they had already forgotten yesterday's massacre.

As the boys walked along with the high grass brushing their rubber shins, it seemed to them that the grass rustled ahead of them, the dry seed-heads swaying and whispering. This was where yesterday they had lain so unsuspectingly.

Presently Tolly called out, 'There's another snake – gone into the bamboo.'

The boys were making for the part where Ping thought Melanie Daisy (as they now called her to reinforce their courage with contempt) had seemed to be, as far as Ping had been able to see in the glass. What was there in the orchard that could have interested her?

'She must have been just about here,' said Ping, leaning on a very old elm tree. 'Oh heavens! Look out, Tolly, it's full of snakes.'

The elm had at some time lost a main fork near the ground. The bark had grown in a thick projecting ring round the cut, and the wood had rotted away inside, leaving a deep hole, partially filled with moss. From this hole three snakes were rearing. Their forked tongues shot in and out as their heads swayed with a menacing alertness.

Tolly and Ping had jumped back out of reach, and as they did so, nearly trod on another that was coiled in the grass and but for its eyes would not have been seen.

They stood stock-still for a moment, afraid to move at all. Then Tolly pulled a torch out of his pocket and, approaching as near as he dared, shone the beam into the hole. The snakes blinked and withdrew a little. Something white glimmered in the moss at the bottom.

'Come and look, Ping. She couldn't have come and filled the hole with snakes' eggs, could she?'

Ping did his best to see, but the snakes were always in movement. They wound their necks and tails round each other, and moved easily and dreadfully in and out of each other's coils, an intricate slippery knot that was never tied; and always their three heads faced the boys. What lay at the bottom of the hole could only be glimpsed.

'Do you think all but one are hatched out already? I wonder how many there were. But these snakes aren't newly hatched. They must be a yard long. It isn't the right time of year for snakes' eggs. Anyway,' said Tolly, 'adders don't lay eggs.'

'Then it is something else she put there and the snakes are guarding it?'

'I suppose so.'

'We ought to get it.'

'Yes.'

Neither boy knew what to do next.

'Let's go round the garden to see if there are lots more. I suppose this is the next plague. She doesn't waste any time.'

They looked carefully round their feet before they moved, wishing their gumboots were waders. The bare patch of knee and thigh exposed between boots and shorts felt very, very bare. Once they were moving again they felt a little braver. They circled the garden, going up and down every path. They even pushed branches aside and peered into thick bushes, and kept a wary eye on overhanging boughs. They saw five more snakes, but the ones they thought had just flickered away were countless.

They found Mrs Oldknow shaking the living-room hearth-rug outside the open door.

'Granny, the garden's full of snakes. If we get bitten, what do we do?'

'We telephone for a car and get into hospital just as quickly as we can, to have a serum injection.'

'Might we be dead?'

'Not if we were quick enough. Leave them alone and they won't hurt you.'

'But, Granny, there are so many of them. We could hardly help treading on them. I very nearly did. One was hanging down out of a tree. They keep their eyes fixed on you.'

'I suppose,' said Ping, 'snakes are the only things Hanno wouldn't like. But he's dead anyway. What difference can it make to him? I've thought of something, Tolly. Wait for me.' He ran upstairs.

Meanwhile Tolly, waiting in the living-room, fiddled with the light switch for no reason except that it was under his finger-tips. The wall light over Mrs Oldknow's chair came on, and as it did so an adder dropped out of the shade. It fell on the back of the chair and glided underneath the cushion. Tolly pulled away the cushion and disclosed a second one lying in wait.

'Granny! There are two snakes in your chair. What shall I do?'

She came and looked in at the door. 'I don't know,' she said, weary but laughing at calamity, 'I really don't. There is no protection against malice. Run round and make sure all the other doors and windows are shut. Upstairs, too, in case they go up the creepers. And leave this door open so that they can go out the way they came in. And if it is me they are looking for, they can follow me to the village, because I am going shopping.'

Ping now came in with something bulky pushed up under his pullover.

'You two had better come with me, I can't leave you here among the adders. In fact, I don't know what to do with you. I'd better make arrangements for you to stay somewhere else until Melanie has exhausted her tricks.'

'No!' said Tolly and Ping together. 'No! And leave you here?'

'And you know it was Ping who got rid of the cats.'

'Well, what *shall* we do?' The old lady sat down on a chair near the door and lifted her feet on to the chair-rail. The boys stood well away to one side. The two adders occupied the armchair and swivelled their heads like machine-guns covering the company.

'I want to try something,' said Ping. 'But please don't go to the village yet, Grand Mother, because we might need your help. Promise.'

'Is that armour you have got under your pullover?'

'Of a sort.'

'Don't do anything dangerous, Ping, please. Though that sounds silly, when even sitting in a chair is dangerous.'

'We have to do *something* about it, don't we, Grand Mother? We can't let Melanie Daisy win. It's your house. The garden really is rustling with snakes. And if they invade the house what can we do? Promise you won't go away till we come back, and then we will be all right.'

With the seriousness of those who volunteer for dangerous missions they set off towards the orchard.

'Is that the Persian glass you've got under your jersey?'

'Yes. I hope it will work.'

Snakes drew arrogantly out of their way as they ran.

When they arrived at the old elm tree, the three snake heads shot up and began their sideways dance.

'Now what, Ping?'

'Hold the glass in front of you and bend down so that they see themselves in it. I hope it will distract their attention. Hold it by your finger-tips – they might get your fingers. But if they bite us, we'll just have to be taken to hospital, that's all. Risks have to be taken.'

Tolly did as suggested. The sun flashed back at the adders out of the glass, and also all the little pieces of glass set in its frame at different angles sparked sun fireworks. The adders were both fascinated and repelled. They did their dance, but now it seemed they were the ones hypnotized. Ping rolled his sleeve back up to his shoulder, then he moved round behind the tree trunk, sliding down till he could reach the snake hole. He folded his pliable fingers and wrist into the shape of a snake's head and quietly plunged his slim yellow arm, which was cold with fright, in among their coils, nuzzling firmly as if he were one of them. Their tails wrapped round it as they did around each other. He felt their muscular pressure. He found the egg and drew it out, then he and Tolly leapt away.

The snakes, after a moment of confusion, slid smoothly and in unison out of the hole and followed them.

Tolly and Ping shot up the ladder into the pear tree.

'I hope they can't climb ladders,' gasped Tolly. He then saw that not only these snakes were waiting for them at the ladder's foot, but more were assembling. They writhed round the lower rungs, rising on their coiled base to raise their heads, which waved like deadly lilies among the grass. Luckily the ladder was aluminium and they could get little purchase on it. 'How do we get down again?' asked Tolly, feeling rather sick.

'One thing at a time,' said Ping. 'It worked, anyway. Now let's see what we've got. It looks like a snake's egg all right. Do something with that glass so that you can have your hands free.'

Tolly, who always looked ahead, held the glass between his knees while he took off his pullover. He put it on the glass so that no one could see what it was. He hung it by its picture wire from the tree. 'If Melanie snoops, it's only half of a dead boy hanging,' he said gruesomely.

He and Ping bent over the egg. It was about the size of a hen's egg, but flabby, except at one end which had a polished, crisper feeling.

'It has been opened and stuck up again with sellotape.'

'We had better open it carefully so that we can put it back again without her noticing anything.'

Ping, with his pocket scissors that last night had cut off his hair, cut the sellotape, and they opened the lid.

Inside there was a dried snakeskin rolled up like a bandage. It had been split all the way down from head to tail, scraped and opened flat. On the inner side there was writing.

'Crossing the River!' cried Tolly, and then clapped a hand over his mouth. Voices travel far from the tops of trees. After that they whispered. They spread the snakeskin out across their knees and studied it.

WONKUOYEMANEHTYBUOYDIB
ISEVOLDLOCYMLIOCSEKANSRE
HTIHEMOC

'It's a foreign language.'
'Try it backwards.'

Come hither snakes, coil my cold loves. I bid you by the Name you know.

'I wish we knew it,' said Tolly. 'What shall we do with the egg now? If we keep it, the adders will stay. And if we destroy it, they might still stay now they are here. Shall we put it in her garden? Then they'll move there. I wonder where she is now. Suppose we could put it in her bed? There might be a window open. Of course she wouldn't mind her cold loves, but I think it would count as a win. Let's try. We can seal it up again. I've got some sellotape in my pocket.'

Ping rolled the skin up on his thigh, and Tolly neatly sealed it in the egg.

At the foot of the ladder the snakes were still trying to climb. By wrapping round each other, some had even reached the third rung.

'We had better take a flying leap from half-way down, and then run.'

They leapt clear of the clustering snakes and as they picked themselves up to run, they saw them disentangle and glide in pursuit. They ran as fast as they could across the rough tussocky grass, made more treacherous by molehills. From the bushes more adders dropped and followed, till the boys felt like terrified snake Pied Pipers. By this time they were near the river and from that part of the garden others were coming to meet them, so that it was no longer possible to keep ahead.

The moment came when Tolly, who was holding the egg, felt a cold touch on the back of his knee. He was too terrified to yell, his voice was paralysed. But no pain followed, and the cold touch was repeated. Ping saw that all the snakes were now gathered round Tolly, who had stopped running, for there were as many in front as behind. Level with the top of the grass, their unblinking eyes, with no expression but awareness, were fixed on Tolly, who stood like a martyr holding his arms above his head. Snakes wound round his gumboots and rubbed their chins softly against his thighs. With far worse horror he realized that this was not hostility but *caresses*. He lowered his arms instinctively, and as the hand holding the egg came down, every craning neck followed its movement and the scaly stroking ceased.

Tolly, beside himself with loathing, hurled the egg with all his might into the river. As he threw, the snakes reared up as high as they could, swaying in the direction of the flight of the egg. Then they sank to the ground for speed, and disappeared. The grass was divided as if a giant comb were being pulled through it and the rustling was as fierce as a hiss. They came into sight again, zigzagging across the river path, which their bodies rubbed with a sound like sandpaper, but as they poured themselves over the bank their gliding into the water made no sound at all. The white egg bobbed conspicuously on the current, carrying its message of 'Come hither, snakes, coil, my cold loves', down the centre of the stream.

Tolly and Ping, released from fear, hopped about on the river path, feeling light enough to fly. As the white egg travelled down past the side of the garden, adders came streaking through the hedge to join those in the water. Though only their heads stuck out, their swimming bodies made the water rough in a new kind of pattern, neither boiling, nor dancing, nor choppy, nor wind-creased, but just thickly alive.

The triumph of Tolly and Ping brought Mrs Old-know out to the gate. They seized her by the arms, one on each side, and hurried her laughing and breathless along the river bank. Ultimately they saw the egg go over the weir, followed by the whole troubled mass of live water.

'The two adders in my armchair left as suddenly as if someone had whistled for them,' the old lady said. 'I went across the lawn to see where you were in the orchard, but all I could see was half of Tolly hanging on the pear tree. Of course Melanie was on the road just there, looking very inquisitive. She seems to prowl round the outside of the place like a rejected lover.'

'Heavens! We forgot the glass.'

They had hardly dared to hope so, but it was still there when they reached the pear tree. If Melanie had meant to take it she must have been distracted by other things. Those who cast spells must surely have a sense of near-panic when their power goes wrong.

The glass was restored to its place in the attic. As the boys went up and down through the house, though they were too polite to look through the window that gave from the Knights' Hall into the spare room, they were aware of Mr Pope working there, and longed to ask him how he was getting on, and if there had been snakes in his ground-floor bedroom. They were glad they had found the book before Melanie had sent the snakes. Otherwise the roof-space might have been full of them.

It was a light-hearted trio that set off at last to go to the village. Needless to say, the talk was about Melanie, what she had done and what she might still do. Each spell of course had to be stronger than the last. It seemed reasonable that it should take longer to prepare. The plague of maggots and the plague of cats had both happened on the same day, the plague of 'adders the day after. But, as Ping said, she probably had lots of those about her all the time. It wouldn't be difficult.

'Except,' Mrs Oldknow suggested, 'that she expends a lot of malice each time, and perhaps like snakes once she has bitten she needs time to recharge. I think we may hope for the rest of today to enjoy ourselves while she brews up something really hard. I do hope she can't do boils. What else could Moses do...? Darkness. Which reminds me – there is to be an eclipse of the sun the day after tomorrow, but that's none of her making.'

'She might find it useful,' Tolly said. 'How long does it last?'

'The whole process about two hours, but the totality hardly a moment. We will get some dark glasses at the shop.'

Ping and Tolly were gay and relaxed. They were not for the moment even worried about what might happen next. They had just done what they could never have believed possible – to plunge one's arm into a nest of adders, to walk in a knot of them. One fear was erased from life for ever and they felt the enlarged freedom.

They needed no entertainment. Simply to be at Green Knowe was occupation enough.

The shape of the house from outside was a perpetual fascination, as simple a block as four walls could be, and yet made up of variations and irregularity, so that each of its four faces was different, but harmonious. It lay in the garden as the Stone of Power once lay among sea ferns in a rock pool. *That* was part of the enclosed mystery and screening of the pool, which was part of the cove in which that stratum of rock lay, which itself was a reciprocal part of the great tides that flowed over it, which were one with the winds and the moon and the sun, which is only a marginal detail of the Milky Way. Just as the Stone of Power held in its nature the truth of all these, so the house of Green Knowe focused in itself and gave out again its own truth about being and knowing.

Something of this kind the boys understood, if only as a feeling of great approval and delight.

Presently they took the clippers and began to trim the yew bushes that were cut into the shape of chessmen, competing with each other in making clean outlines. That done, they lay on the grass and watched the ocean-going clouds sail slowly across.

Inevitably during the morning Melanie went past. The river path was the direct way from her house to the village. She leant over the gate, near which they lay chewing grass stalks.

'Good morning, boys. Just lying about on the grass! You seem to be having rather a dull holiday.'

They got to their feet, partly because politeness dies hard, partly because it is better to meet an enemy standing.

'It hasn't been really dull,' said Tolly.

'An old lady isn't much fun for two lively boys. Just fetching and carrying for her, I dare say, and listening to old talk.'

Neither boy spoke, so she went on, 'If you cared to help me in a little experiment I am doing, I think you would find it exciting. Just the sort of thing boys really like, especially over-grandmothered boys with plenty of originality like you. Are you doing anything this afternoon?'

'What time, please?' said Ping, meaning only to keep her talking.

'Just before sundown. You simply slip away without saying anything, bringing *you know what* with you. It will be necessary for the experiment. And then we will have my peep-show.'

'What shall we see?' asked Ping, as casual as the most wicked conspirator.

For a moment she seemed to turn over various baits in her mind, and then she whispered:

'An execution.'

'Whose?' said Ping, in the same dead-pan voice.

She laughed uncontrollably, higher and higher. 'Not just *anybody's*. Oh, no. Not just anybody. You'll see. You'll like it. But I have a lot to do first. I must go and get ready. Be sure you bring *you-know-what*.'

They watched her till she was out of sight.

'She is too disgusting,' said Tolly. 'Does she mean the book or the glass by you-know-what?'

'She doesn't know herself what it is, only that we had something in the orchard. Should we go now?'

'Where?' asked Tolly.

'To The Firs. We might see something. She won't be back for a long time.'

'Yes,' Tolly agreed stoutly. 'She is a hyena woman, a leopard woman, a werewolf woman, a harpy, a beast, a bluebottle. I don't know any words bad enough. I hate her.'

They went along to The Firs and in boldly at the gate. The washing line of birds was still there. They had to bend to pass under it. No one could come in without doing so. It was a degrading gesture of submission to beastliness.

The garden was not only neglected, it gave the impression of being fouled and blasted. A bonfire smouldered in the middle of the grass, giving off a bad smell of burning offal. The surrounding hedge was curled and singed, the grass trampled. There were no flowers. It might have been a back yard in the saddest part of London instead of next-door neighbour to Green Knowe under the same endlessly varying sky.

The house itself was a pleasant building, but was repellent in that every window was shut and every curtain drawn across from top to bottom. It did not look like a house of the dead, still less that of an over-careful person who dreads sun fading when the rooms are not in use. What was powerfully suggested was that the curtains were drawn so that whatever was inside should not be seen looking out.

The boys warily circled the house. Every door and window was locked back and front. No messages were pinned on the door for laundry or greengrocery. No milk bottles stood outside. It was clear that except for Melanie nobody ever came to the house. Its blind eyes got on the boys' nerves.

They stepped back into the grass for a general survey, and Tolly then noticed that the bonfire was smouldering on top of a large stone slab very slightly raised. Ping came over to look, and pointed out, a little way behind it, a hole in the turf bigger and deeper than a golf hole, as if some fixture slotted into it.

'We can't get into the house without breaking a window. And then she would know. Besides, we might let something out by mistake. Whatever those other boys saw. We might look in that shed. The door is broken.'

The shed was a lean-to, only a little way from the front door. The boys opened the groaning broken door and took a step in, but the door swung shut behind them, this time with a screech, and they were in almost total darkness with their hair standing on end, they didn't know why. Ping quickly pushed the door half open and blocked it with the first thing that came to hand, which was nothing more alarming than an old hand mower. They then had light to look around.

It was a deep shed full of throw-outs such as every established house has. It had a dusty musty smell and long flapping cobwebs. A large grandiose shape was the first to be recognized – an ancient bath chair filling up the opening. The familiar element in the mustiness was now traced, the smell of mildewed leather cushions, of the chequered oilcloth foot-rest, of perishing rubber tyres, clogged oil and the rather nasty metal smell of brass. There was nothing about this brooding old relic to inspire the horror they felt in here. Of course bath chairs are sometimes used for moving nodding old near-corpses about. And could be used for corpses. But the boys disregarded the bath chair and looked further. There was a fat toad sitting in a corner. Above it hung an outsize skein of raffia. No. Not just raffia. Half hidden by it was a small and dreadful whited mask, from which the raffia hung like hair, long enough and thick enough to dress anyone who wore it. The smallness of the face would make the wearer look very tall, and it was wizened into unspeakable meanness.

This was shaking enough, and yet the boys' instincts or antennae still expected something worse. They were goose-fleshed and their thumbs were pricking.

It was the ordinariness of this other thing that for a long time prevented them from seeing it. Among the ladders, toothless rakes and wooden curtain rods, a simple pole like a laundry prop. But it had two goats' horns stuck in the top. Tolly saw the shadow of the

horns on the wall before he saw the real thing. They recognized it at once as absolutely evil.

Ping at last screwed his way in behind the bath chair for a closer look. Winding round the pole all the way up was a shallowly incised irregular pattern.

'It's "Crossing the River", of course. I'll spell it out, Tolly, and you write it down, and then we'll get out of here. I don't like it.'

The writing was not only backward, it was awiddershins, that is, turning round the pole in the opposite direction from the sun. But Ping read it out from the top downward, touching the pole only enough to twist it round. Tolly wrote down the apparently meaningless letters,

LAILEBDROLDNAREHPSOHP
ANOGROGOMEDENISULEM.

By the time they had finished they were both sweating and shaking, and Ping looked ghastly. They ran as if for their lives, and at last flung themselves panting on the sweet grass at Green Knowe.

It was a long time before either of them spoke.

'I don't want to know what it says,' said Tolly at last.

'We shall have to look. You didn't throw it away?'

'No. The beastly thing is in my pocket.'

'The pole would fit the socket on her lawn.'

'Oh, shut up. I suppose the execution would have been one of us.'

'I wonder what I could wash in after touching that thing.'

'Let's go to Grand.'

'Do you know what I thought, from what she said? I thought she was going to make us look in the glass and see something frightful happen to Grand Mother. She does hate her so. But I suppose we are at least as bad as the birds. Bad enough to be got rid of.'

They found Mrs Oldknow sitting in the inner garden with one of the patchwork quilts over her knees. She was unpicking torn patches and putting in new ones.

Tolly, who had an intimate knowledge of these quilts, stood by her.

'That's Susan's nightdress you're taking out,' he said.

'Yes, alas. Someone at the laundry has put a finger right through it.'

Ping wanted to know who Susan was.

'She lived here as a child in the eighteenth century. She was blind, but very lively and intelligent and her father's darling. Tolly has seen her sometimes, which is not odd, because this is her house as well as his, and sometimes, naturally enough, she is in it.'

'You've taken out all her bits,' Tolly said regretfully. 'Now she won't be in the patchwork any more.'

'Well, naturally all the bits of the same stuff go rotten at the same time – the time it takes to do it. Gather up the scraps please, Tolly my dear. Put them in the bin that is waiting to be emptied by the gate.'

Tolly picked up the torn and faded remnants of Susan and took them down to the road where the bins of the nearest houses were standing waiting to be emptied. He lifted the lid of the Green Knowe bin and put the scraps in it. As he was returning up the drive, he heard the bin lid lifted again, and turned round to look. 'I might have known,' he said to himself. 'Snoop, snoop, snoop. Why does she want to know what we put in our bins?'

*

He joined Ping and his great-grandmother again. Ping had been telling her about their exploration at The Firs. In her presence nothing was ever quite so frightening. Tolly brought out his pocket-book, and together they considered the letters that had been carved up the pole.

LAILEBDROLDNAREHPSOHPANOGRO
GOMEDENISULEM.

Beginning from the end it made not much better sense.

MELUSINEDEMOGORGONAPHOSPHERA
NDLORDBELIAL

The old lady put down her sewing to look. 'Well, at least we know the last word, BELIAL.'

'What does it mean?' asked Ping.

'One of the names of Satan.'

'Would she say LORD BELIAL?'

'I'm sure she would.'

'Then it ends "and Lord Belial",' Tolly read triumphantly. 'Now we will begin at the beginning. Does MELUS mean anything?'

'Not that I know of. But Melusine is a name. She was the devil's daughter.'

'If we are looking for monsters, there's Gorgon later on. She had snakes. But DEMO comes in between.'

'We are certainly keeping bad company,' the old lady said. 'Demogorgon is another of the devil's names. He naturally has a great many, being a many-sided fellow.'

'That only leaves APHOSPHER.'

'Phospher is the Greek for Lucifer.'

'MELUSINE DEMOGORGONA PHOSPHER AND LORD

BELIAL,' Ping read out. 'M. D. P. Melanie Delia Powers. It's her true secret name.'

'And her true secret profession,' Mrs Oldknow added.

'You were wrong, Grand Mother, about her needing time like a snake to store up more venom. It pumps through her all the time with her blood. It never stops. She is busy doing something horrible now, but it won't come off, because we shan't go. She expects us at sundown.'

'I think now we know her true name we may have the upper hand. But don't go there again, my dears.'

The sunset was a fine fiery one. Dropping through a geranium-coloured sky, it looked exactly what it was, a stupendous fire blazing in space. Its long spokes of light pierced between the branches, lit up the boles of trees, turned brick walls into a festival glow and the glossy leaves of evergreens into sun candles. Every bush and flower stood up and was bathed in the sun's colour. It streamed into the house, filling it with glory. It painted the shape of the Norman windows on the stone of the opposite wall and woke a lively response in the smooth surfaces of glass or wood or basket. It was hard to believe that such magnificence could be eclipsed by a little wandering moon. It set behind The Firs, which showed as a mere dark obstacle, huddled and unwilling.

It was not until the splendid display was over and the colours had gone cold, that anyone remembered the enemy. What had she meant to do? What would she do now? The remembered shudders began to creep up Tolly's spine again. He looked at Ping, whose face was inscrutably thoughtful. Both boys were very tired when they went up to bed.

Tolly looked in the Persian glass as they always did. He stood in front of it for a minute smiling and surprised and then called out to Ping, 'Do you know who I saw in it? Susan! I must be dreaming awake. Anyway, I like seeing Susan. She belongs here.' He flung himself into bed and rolled over.

Ping looked in the glass. 'I can't see anything. Oh dear, I wish Melanie would go. Tolly? We could make a spell with her secret name.'

But Tolly was asleep. Ping put out the light. It was a night of almost absolute darkness. The moon would not rise for hours yet. Ping sighed. Then he too slept.

Tolly's sleep, however, was troubled. There was a patchwork quilt on his bed similar to the one Mrs Oldknow had been mending. Tonight it kept slipping off, and not just when he turned over, but in jerks as if someone were pulling it.

He had been dreaming about the cakes that moved, except that in his dream the cakes were something different and terribly important. He was awakened by the rustle and thud of his quilt sliding on to the floor. Something was going on. Someone was in the room, moving about carefully and slowly, with unnatural uncertainty. To his ears came a small sound, hardly more than lips opening and closing on a breath, and yet it was a sound of distress.

His quilt, by the drag of it, was in movement on the floor, and someone seemed to stumble on it. There was a long pause, and then a noise of quite a different quality, loud and startling. Yet it was only the Persian mirror sliding a little from side to side on the plaster wall by his ear. What could make it do that? There followed a metal twang such as the wire would make if it fell loose against the frame. If the wire broke the glass should fall. But the glass did not fall.

Tolly was now sitting up, feeling entirely made of the sharpest of senses. The light switch was by Ping's bed. Tolly reached out to touch the mirror where it should be hanging. Its place was empty. He strained his eyes in the darkness, and saw that a square of not-dark, of remote silver half-gleam that the mirror always somehow picked up from somewhere, was sidling about the room like a will-o'-the-wisp.

Tolly got up and followed.

At the door which opened on to the attic stairs, that little unhappy sound came again and bare feet padded, feeling for the stairs. For a moment his hands met the frame of the mirror.

'Don't pull,' said Susan's voice. 'You will make me fall. Let go.'

It was true that with both hands to carry the glass, she could not use the stair-rail, and the winding stairs were almost ladder-steep.

Tolly followed the hesitant will-o'-the-wisp down to the Knights' Hall. From the shuttered window behind which Mr Pope worked, a shaft of light crossed the room. Through this Susan passed, showing for a moment a face of such unhappiness that Tolly's heart smote him. He could not possibly wrench the glass from her by violence. He laid his hand on it.

'Susan! Susan! It's me, Tolly. Where are you going? Give me the glass.'

'Leave me alone. I am to take it to the lady at the garden gate. Leave me. Let me go.' She made those whimpering almost animal sounds that children make in their sleep during nightmares.

At that moment there was a kind of waterfall down the stairs. Tolly's bed quilt had joined them.

'Don't pull my nightgown.'

'I'm not touching you,' said Tolly.

'Somebody's pulling me. I have to give this thing to a lady —'

'Give it to me,' said Tolly, 'in the name of Melusine Demogorgona Phosper.'

There was a wild cry, and sobbing that died away on the air. The Persian glass was heavy in Tolly's hands.

Tolly was almost equally unhappy. He went into Mrs Oldknow's room and sat on her bed wrapped in her summer eiderdown while he told her.

'Do you think I did Susan any harm by using that beastly name to her?'

'No, my dear. I think you relieved her of doing what she didn't want to do. I think she cried because it was so horrid and now it was over.'

She handed Tolly a tin of biscuits that she kept by her bed for sleepless nights.

'I don't want to go back to bed yet, because the quilt is lying there. Just the other side of this door. Can Melanie have wanted to get at me?'

Mrs Oldknow sat up considering. Huddled in bed, Tolly thought she looked like some funny little wise tree animal, bright-eyed and quick. But also her company was infinitely reassuring.

'I think,' she said at last, 'there is some of Susan's nightdress in your quilt as well as in the one I mended today. What did you do with the bits?'

'I put them in the bin. Oh, yes – Melanie was snooping around.'

'That's it then. She used the bits to call up Susan, or at least *someone* from the house. And the quilt came too. I think you will find it quite inert now. But I'll come with you.'

She put on her dressing-gown and slippers. Her cobwebby white hair was tousled and childlike.

'Melanie must ask herself what in the world I've got in here. She doesn't think enough of you two. You are a couple of tough young obstacles.'

A whole day had passed, after that last attempt to get the glass, without sight or sound of Miss Powers or any unusual happening at Green Knowe. The boys and Mrs Oldknow, after so many shocks and alarms, could hardly believe in the lovely ordinariness. The relief made them very ready to be amused. Their chuckles and trills, exploding jokes and gales of laughter spread through the house and garden and cleared the air. The helpless silliness of boys aching with laughter delighted the old lady. It had an artless and absolute excellence. She marvelled at their ability to take the moment as it came. In one way, their laughter was the measure of their anxiety. Between every joke there was room for a ghost of fear on which they turned their backs.

Mr Pope too had been happily engaged. He could be heard humming to himself as he turned the pages, reading passages aloud, or congratulating himself as a missing word was fitted in. When he passed the boys on the stairs he smiled approvingly at them and told them he had nearly finished piecing together an important passage called the Invocation of Power. He seemed quite to have forgotten the existence of Melanie Powers. To him it was a question of scholarship relating to the ninth century or earlier, pursued with great acumen among the clues, the remnants and the gaps of lost time, but having no connection with the passions of one's next-door neighbour.

The boys had been concocting a plan of their own against Melanie D. Powers. It had needed rehearsing, and as they tried it out in the attic it was found to offer much variety to their dramatic talent. This also provoked high spirits, because an actor believes entirely in what he does and never doubts that it will have the prearranged result. The end of the play is known. But though throughout the afternoon and evening they had hung about the river path, there had been no sign at all of the enemy.

Today there was to be the eclipse of the sun, to be total at nine in the morning. The boys therefore were up early. Breakfast was to be finished by eight, so that the first bite into the sun's disc could be watched.

The perfect weather continued and the boys, leaning out of their top window, saw the sun rise in a clear golden sky. There were a few patches of trailing mist, which seemed to thicken to a low fog around The Firs and trail thinly from there toward Green Knowe. The air had a sharp edge which made the scents fresher to breathe as ice improves the taste of drinks.

The boys did not omit to look in the Persian glass, where at first they saw nothing but a swirl of mist, and then, as clear as if the glass were held near her in a room, the white face of Melanie Powers, eyes closed and teeth bared in the desperate grin of people exerting their last strength. 'She's dead!' cried Tolly. But they could see by her nostrils that she was not dead, only lost in a supreme effort.

'Crikey! What's coming to us this time?'

The boys felt suddenly altogether disheartened. Since dawn they had been preparing with unquestioning enthusiasm to carry out their device, but now they lost confidence in it.

Ping, however, remarked for their encouragement that the glass appeared to be increasing in power. It was no longer confined to reflecting the place where it hung, but had shown them Melanie not in any particular place, but just herself.

They went downstairs feeling like people about to sit for an examination. However, their uneasiness was forgotten when Mrs Oldknow welcomed them waving a cable. 'Tolly darling, news for you! Your father is flying back from Burma and will be here tomorrow. "Bringing a friend," is all he says.' She put her arm round Ping's shoulders, because she knew he would be wishing it could be his father, of whom he had heard nothing for years. He believed him to have been killed in those old days of guerrilla warfare when he himself had become a refugee.

The cable had been delivered by the postman with the letters. He had rung the bell twice, and after handing in the cable had asked Mrs Oldknow to come out and see what was on the door.

'I wouldn't care to have such a thing nailed on my house, ma'am. I should tell the police if I were you. That's not teenage stuff. It's real nasty.'

On the centre of the door, nailed with four tacks, was hanging what looked like the palm side of a child's leather glove. But it was paper-stiff like dried skin, and showed the lines of a real hand. Across the palm was written:

RUIN FALL ON YOU

Mrs Oldknow felt very sick.

'For God's sake pull it off,' she said. 'I can't let the boys see that. It's abominable.'

The postman reluctantly got out his pocket knife and prised up the tacks one by one. The hand swung on the last one and then slithered down to the ground. 'I wouldn't touch it, ma'am, if I were you,' the postman said, getting on his bicycle and riding off.

'It's a question of what you believe is strongest,' she answered. But she stood there nonplussed.

At last she went in and brought back one of those venerable much-used prayer books that old ladies have, with which all their lives they have tried to put good

before evil. It fell open at the most-read passage. Between those pages she put the defiled, innocent hand and closed the book on it. She then bound it round and round with sellotape in both directions, as if staunching a deep wound. The book would never be opened again. What to do with it now? She took it round and hid it behind St Christopher in the depths of his ivy and Traveller's Joy.

She had just done this when she heard the boys laying the table. She hid her fear from them and they did the same for her. There was the cable to talk about. She had had a letter from Tolly's father some weeks before, saying that he might have to fly to England for a short visit on business. It was most lucky that this should happen before Tolly went back to school.

Before the chatter of breakfast was over, the glory of the morning had begun to dim. They took their dark glasses and went up on to the balcony at the door of the Knights' Hall, from which they could most easily watch the sun, not yet as high as the tree-tops. This balcony was once the head of an outside staircase leading from the garden to what was then the main entrance. The doorway was Norman, and the wall above it the most weather-worn corner of the house. It had a pronounced outward lean, as many old walls have, and had been much patched. It was buttressed by the remains of the old chapel.

When Mrs Oldknow and the boys took their stand here, they were in full warm sun. The old stone wall against which they leant was warm to the touch. Red admirals sunned their wings on it and overhead, seen against the sky, the bees in the roof peacefully came and went. Below them was the inner garden, deep and green like a garden at the bottom of a lake.

In the house behind them Mr Pope was at work as always. Coincidences in the orbits of sun and moon were no more to him than the turn of the calendar year. He was busy, and the universe could go on its appointed way. He was at the climax of his piecing together and did not notice the outside conditions. When, later on, the sun failed, he grumbled and automatically turned on the electricity.

As the shape of the moon began to cut off one side of the sun, the first birds to be disturbed by it were the swallows, whose twittering as they lined up on the telephone cables sounded like an excited parliament. Had they left their flight till too late?

Minute by minute the world grew darker, and the other birds, who had thought the day was just beginning, began to call danger. Because this was not even dusk. The sun had not gone down; it was failing in mid-heaven. The bees buzzed fretfully round their entrance under the roof, some trying to come out, others anxious to get in again.

A brooding greenish half-dark, suggesting thunderstorms, was gathering steadily, yet instead of heat there came a sickly cold that was neither of night nor of winter, but a presage of death. The cows on the island mooed in long uneasy question-marks and moved about in a procession to nowhere. The horses whinnied and clustered together, and the birds were in full panic.

As totality approached, silence fell over the frightened earth. Tolly, holding up a smoked glass to reinforce his dark spectacles, saw the weird disc of the sun jumping to his own heart-beats. *There was something else*. He glanced wildly round, at a loss, not knowing in which direction he should look, or for what. A loud buzzing from the bees in the roof drew his eyes upward. Was it the pale bellies of a crowd of tits squeezing up between the tiles? He pulled off his sun-glasses and looked again. He pulled Ping's sleeve and pointed, speechless.

What were those *things* working about at the lower edge of the roof just above their heads? It was almost too dark to see, but they looked like fingers, without hand or arm. Fingers of some dreadful unknown substance, sub-physical or super-physical, projectile grey matter. If hatred could be seen at work, it might look like that. Whatever it was, it worked forcefully and wickedly. As the boys looked, a shower of tiles slithered down the slope in a roar of bees, and the fingers moved on and were prising at the top corner-stone of the leaning wall. Tolly and Ping dragged Mrs Oldknow into the house just as the big chiselled stone was dislodged and fell where she had been standing. The shuddering moment of horror as the sun disappeared was accompanied by a shower of heavy stones hitting the rail of the balcony and bouncing into the garden.

Mrs Oldknow, for once heart-broken beyond any possible action, could only say, 'If it is coming down, you had better be outside.' She sank on a seat and hid her face, and the boys would not leave her.

'Are you wearing the Stone?' asked Tolly.

'Yes, I always do. But I can't help remembering that the last person who wore it was driven into the sea.'

At this moment they heard from the spare room the

voice of Mr Pope dictating into his tape recorder. His voice rose and fell in a Latin chant and reigned over a silence that was sudden and absolute like a crack in Time. Then, as he continued, the house shook as when the sound barrier is broken. A stone crashed on the roof of the old chapel. Mr Pope's voice came louder. The sonorous words rolled out, and it was clear that he called upon secret and mighty names.

Ping and Tolly, awestruck and holding their breath, saw the powerful white fingers fall one by one on to the balcony, wriggle, snatch and evaporate into puffs of retreating fog.

Here is a translation of the Invocation of Power, which Mr Pope was so splendidly declaiming:

Powers of the Kingdom be beneath my left foot and within my right hand.

Glory and Eternity touch my shoulders and guide me in the paths of victory.

Mercy and Judgment be ye the equilibrium and splendour of my life.

BINAHEL be thou my love.

Be thou that which thou art and that which thou willest to be, Oh KETHERIEL.

CHERUBIM be my strength in the name of ADONAI.

ELOHIM fight for me in the name of TETRAGRAMMA-TON.

MALACHIM protect me in the name of YOD HE VAN HE.

ARALIM, act ye.

AUPHANIM, revolve and shine.

CHAIOTH, HAQUADOSH, cry aloud, speak, roar and groan.

QUADOSCH,	QUALOSCH,	QUADOSCH
SHADDAI,	ADONAI,	YOD.
CHAVAH,	E HE IEH	
ASHER	E HE IEH	
HALLELU	YAH	

During the last part of this, a wailing of lost and time-less despair moved across the garden, pursued by Mr Pope's triumphant E he ieh, drawn out like a long bugle note.

Absolute silence followed. Mrs Oldknow and the two boys hurried outside to see how much damage had been done. The totality of eclipse was over, but it was still as dark as a winter dawn. They could see a hole in the roof, the rafters sagging free where the top corner of the massive wall had gone. The balcony was broken. Stones lay about on the grass. Luckily they had fallen clear of St Christopher's head. The stone child on his shoulder still held up its baby hand unbroken, blessing the darkness.

The old lady sighed, thinking of that other hand.

'No more harm done here than can be repaired,' she said at last.

Tolly and Ping, seeing that she was all right again, kissed her quickly and ran off to carry out their plan. Each stuffed in the front of his pullover a foot-long cardboard roll such as calenders are posted in. They crossed the garden, weird and restless in the lop-sided morning dawn, and made for the big elms beside the river path where it was almost certain that their victim must sooner or later pass.

*

It was a quarter to one by the church clock before their ambush was rewarded. From their hiding-place in the branches of the thickest elm, they saw Melanie tottering across the field. Her strange walk was both rapid and unwilling, suggesting somebody holding her by the collar and pushing her on. As she came nearer they could see that she was hard hit. She was drawn and haggard, as if, as Tolly said later, all the stuffing had gone out of her, but whatever force drove her on was relentless.

Just before she came under the tree, the boys put their cardboard trumpets to their lips and a hollow, hardly audible whisper floated out.

Avaunt! Hence, begone! Melusine Demogórgona Phóspher!

At 'Melusine' she stopped dead to listen, looking round for the source of the sound.

Vaunt! Hence, begone! Melusine Demogorgona Phospher!
Hence, begone! Melusine Demogorgona Phospher!
Begone! Melusine Demogorgona Phospher!
Gone! Melusine Demogorgona Phospher!
MELUSINE DEMOGORGONA PHOSPHER.
You seen Demogorgona Phospher?
Seen Demogorgona Phospher.
DEMOGORGONA PHOSPHER!
Oh! Gorgona Phospher!
Gorgona Phospher!
Gone, Ah! Phospher.
Ah! Phospher!
Phospher!
pher!

All this time she grew more agitated. She was by now

underneath the tree, partly hidden from them by the lower branches, and as Tolly gave the final 'pher!' she was contorted into a kind of wrestling match with herself, crying out 'Don't leave me' in a voice like wood rending.

'E he ieh,' came down Tolly's trumpet.

With a last convulsion the writhing form, now on the ground, broke up into two. Melanie lay sobbing, and an abomination that the mind refuses to acknowledge stood over her and spurned her, and sped away hidden by a line of hedge.

The boys gripped the branches, speechless and near to fainting, afraid their hearts would never start beating again.

Melanie dragged herself up. She was now known, exposed, a failure, and cast off by her demon lord. An empty, powerless woman, crumpled up and distracted. She ran about like a hen, but finally turned again towards the old magnet of her cupidity, Green Knowe. She went hesitantly, her thumbs and little fingers stuck out as if nervously keeping something away.

Tolly and Ping, still shaken, came down and followed at a distance.

Mrs Oldknow and Mr Pope were standing outside looking up at the damaged wall and debating the possibility of cause and effect, and how much they dared admit to themselves what they believed. When Melanie come round the corner Mrs Oldknow found that harder to believe than anything else. This popeyed, huddled woman with her little fingers like snails' horns and her air of not knowing what she had come for, was this the ruthless adversary they had been supposing?

She advanced with her hesitant hen steps, knowing she was unwanted, knowing she would be rejected.

'It's turned out quite nice after the eclipse, hasn't it?' she said, as nobody spoke. She drew near the leaning corner of the house. The wall was raw like a cliff when boulders have slipped. Loose stones still balanced there precariously. Melanie gaped at it.

'Can I help you?' said Mr Pope, who had not met her before and did not guess who she was. 'What do you want?'

She heard his voice, and blinked rapidly, showing the whites of her eyes.

'I've lost my Cat.' She turned and scurried away. 'I've lost ...'

For the last time the boys watched her going away down the garden path – nervous, running, stumbling, diminishing. The gate clicked.

ENVOY

'Now we can take the witchball upstairs again,' said Tolly. 'She didn't mind passing it this time, since she has lost her Cat. I am glad none of the stones hit this.'

He and Ping took it up to their room and hung it from its nail, where it swung softly before settling into sleep.

'We can take the Persian glass down to its proper place too,' said Ping. 'Though it is wasted there with nothing to reflect except Time.'

He put his hands on the frame and looked casually and gaily into it. Across the room, Tolly saw his friend's face change into something so sad, desperate and disbelieving that he could hardly believe it was the boy he knew.

'Oh, no!' he cried, 'she *can't* come back.' He flew to Ping's side to see what he was seeing. They both stared.

'Is it, is it, is it?' gasped Ping.

'Yes, it is,' said Tolly, then with a sudden bound of inspiration, he added, 'Is it?'

'Yes, it is!'

They hugged and thumped each other. They went helter-skelter and clattered down the stairs, thundered across the resounding floor of the Knights' Hall and flung themselves to slide down the banister-rail, shouting, Granny! and Grand Mother! in high voices. She came laughing. 'Don't shake the house too much. It's still feeling rather weak. What is it?'

'It's – it's – it's –' stammered Ping, and could get no further.

'It's Ping's father! Daddy's friend is Ping's father. We have seen them in the glass coming in together at the garden gate.'

And so it was.

Some other Puffins

DOLPHIN ISLAND
Arthur C. Clarke

Johnny Clifton had never been happy living with Aunt Martha and her family for the twelve years since his parents had died when he was four. So when an intercontinental hovership breaks down outside his house, he stows away on it.

THE WITCHES
Roald Dahl

No silly hats and broomsticks here! This is a book about 'real' witches – those that absolutely loathe children and are always plotting to get rid of them. A Whitbread Award winner.

CHARLIE LEWIS PLAYS FOR TIME
Gene Kemp

Cricklepit Combined School, which produced Tyke Tiler and endured Gowie Corby, is now coping with five of the numerous Moffat family. Trish and the others find they have a new teacher for their last term at Cricklepit, a strict disciplinarian who believes in silence, segregation and sex discrimination. But for one member of the family the worst thing is that Mr Carter has a passion for music.

WOOF! *Allan Ahlberg*

Eric is a perfectly ordinary boy. Perfectly ordinary, that is, until the night when, safely tucked up in bed, he slowly turns into a dog! Fritz Wegner's drawings illustrate this funny and exciting story superbly.

VERA PRATT AND THE FALSE MOUSTACHES
Brough Girling

There were times when Wally Pratt wished his mum was more ordinary and not the fanatic mechanic she was, but when he and his friends find themselves caught up in a real 'cops and robbers' affair, he is more than glad to have his mum, Vera, to help them.

SADDLEBOTTOM *Dick King-Smith*

Hilarious adventures of a Wessex Saddleback pig whose white saddle is in the wrong place, to the chagrin of his mother.

A TASTE OF BLACKBERRIES *Doris Buchanan Smith*

The moving story about a young boy who has to come to terms with the tragic death of his best friend and the guilty feeling that he could somehow have saved him.